Gulf Coast Cottage

Blackbird Beach, book one

Maggie Miller

Maggie Miller

GULF COAST COTTAGE: Blackbird Beach, book 1
Copyright © 2021 Maggie Miller

All rights reserved. No part of this book may be reproduced in any form or by any electronic or mechanical means, including information storage and retrieval systems—except in the case of brief quotations embodied in critical articles or reviews—without permission in writing from the author.

This book is a work of fiction. The characters, events, and places portrayed in this book are products of the author's imagination and are either fictitious or are used fictitiously. Any similarity to real person, living or dead, is purely coincidental and not intended by the author.

Gulf Coast Cottage

Escape to the Gulf Coast of Florida with Georgia Carpenter as she gets a second chance at life, love, and happiness.

In the middle of an awful divorce, fifty-three-year-old Georgia Carpenter finds herself out of luck, time, and money. Then her phone rings with the news that her great aunt has died and left her a cottage in the Gulf Coast town of Blackbird Beach.

Georgia has no idea what awaits her on the other coast of Florida. All she knows is that she has nowhere else to go. And no reason to stay where she is.

Fortunately for her, life has far more interesting plans than she ever could have realized. Including making the acquaintance of a handsome handyman and getting the chance at a brand-new start.

Maggie Miller

Chapter One

With her phone pressed to her ear, Georgia Carpenter stared blankly into her tiny studio apartment. Nothing before her really registered. Not the mess of taped up boxes, or the garbage bags full of clothes, or the random assortment of suitcases and reusable shopping totes all stuffed to the brim with her earthly belongings.

All of her energy, what was left of it, was focused on trying to process what the attorney, a Mr. Roger Gillum, was telling her on the other end of the line.

"My great aunt Norma?" Georgia had only ever thought of her as Aunt Norma, but she was technically a great. In many ways.

"Yes, ma'am. She passed away at the end of July. I'm very sorry for your loss. If we could schedule a time for you to come into our office to go over her will—"

"But she was only in her seventies." Georgia had been meaning to go visit Norma for ages, but with the divorce and losing the house and having to move, and now having to move again, well, life had gotten in the way. Georgia sighed, filled with sadness that her aunt was gone. And had been for nearly three months now.

"Ma'am, Norma Merriweather was eighty-nine."

"She was?" Georgia put a hand to her head, doing some quick math. Of course that's how old Norma had been because there had always been a thirty-six-year age difference between them, and Georgia was fifty-three.

"Yes, ma'am."

She was also a terrible grandniece for not visiting. Terrible. "Yes, I suppose she was."

"We've overnighted you the package with the—"

"Oh, that was from you?" She'd gotten a package this morning but hadn't opened it. All she'd seen was the name of an attorney in the address section and figured it was more divorce paperwork that she didn't have time to deal with. Besides, she was trying to get her belongings together. That was all that mattered in the moment.

"Yes. We sent you the deed information and the keys to the—"

"Keys?" And he'd said deed. That implied property. New hope sprung up inside her. "Did she leave me a house?"

"Yes. A cottage—"

"The one on Sea Glass Lane?" Georgia had always loved that little bungalow. Although she hadn't been there in years. No telling what shape it was in now. Although, inherited meant free, and beggars, such as she was about to become, couldn't be choosers. "She left that to me? That's amazing."

"Yes, ma'am, she did. Now, if you could just let me explain." He hesitated like he was expecting her to cut him off again.

"I will. But not right now." For one thing, he was using up her minutes and she was already woefully low on those. For another, she had to be out by five and she hadn't even started to pack the car yet. "I'll call you in a few days, I promise, but I have some life stuff going that I have to deal with first. Legal stuff." Like losing her lease. "You're a lawyer, I'm sure you understand that, right?"

"Well, yes, but this really can't—"

"Great. Thanks for understanding. Talk soon, Mr. Gillum. Bye." She hung up, tucked the phone into the back pocket of her denim shorts and picked up the package she'd received earlier. She tore the strip off the top and dumped the contents onto her kitchen counter.

A heavy set of keys clunked out.

She snorted. "How many keys do you need for a cottage?"

But maybe there was a different one for the back door, too. And maybe another for a storage shed. Hard to say. Didn't matter. She'd figure it out tonight when she got there. Right now, she had to pack the last few boxes of her stuff, load all of it into her Pathfinder and pray that the old SUV would make the four-hour drive to Blackbird Beach.

The quaint little town was on the other side of the state and a little below the much more bustling tourist destination of St. Pete's Beach, a true Florida resort.

Blackbird Beach had never really achieved that status due to some old timey laws that strictly controlled all of the building that went on in town. Laws Aunt Norma had probably helped pass. As a result, the little town had been left mostly unspoiled. If Georgia remembered right, there were only a few B&Bs in town and no big hotels or even high-rise condo buildings. They just weren't allowed.

Whatever, didn't matter, Georgia had nowhere else to go. She'd run out of money and couldn't afford even this tiny, worn out studio anymore. The home baking business she'd tried to get going, making cakes and cupcakes, had been doing all right until she'd moved into this studio. The tiny kitchen just made that kind of baking impossible.

But the studio had been all she'd been able to afford. And after years of being out of the workforce to focus on being a mom and housewife, she'd struggled to find a decent job.

Divorce was fun like that. Thankfully, her son and daughter were grown now and able to take care of themselves or she really would have been in a bad way.

Muttering the name of her ex under her breath along with a few other choice words, she went back to work. There wasn't much to do but pack her remaining clothes and toiletries, then fill the cooler with the few perishables still in the fridge. After that, she had to load everything into the car.

An hour and a half later, she was done. Sweaty and exhausted but done. She'd gotten everything to fit, too, which was great, but also a sad commentary about how little she owned. She paused for a moment, wondering if she should take a hot shower while she had the chance. There was no telling what she'd find at the cottage. It might not even have water.

But showering now would mean unpacking the toiletries she'd just packed. And finding new clothes to put on. She didn't have the energy. Or the time. It was a couple minutes after five now and there was no telling when the landlord would be by to see if she was out.

She got behind the wheel of her Pathfinder, said a little prayer that it would make the journey, then stuck the key in the ignition.

She was about to start the engine when her phone rang. She checked the screen. It was Mia, her daughter. Georgia answered right away. "Hi, honey."

"Mom," Mia sobbed. Then she dissolved into the kind of crying that made words impossible to understand.

Georgia went into panic and protect mode. "Honey, what's wrong? Are you hurt? Were you in an accident? I can't understand you."

"Brendan," she managed to get out. "I caught him cheating on me. With Sarah, of all people!"

Georgia's mouth dropped open. Mia and Brendan had only just gotten engaged a few months ago. It had been the one bright spot in the dark and devastating divorce Georgia had been going through.

And Sarah was supposed to be Mia's Maid of Honor. So much for that. "Oh, honey. Oh, I'm so sorry. What can I do?"

"Can I come stay with you? I can't stay here."

Mia lived in Palm Beach, a much more metropolitan part of Florida a few hours south of Georgia. "I would love to have you—"

"Great. I already packed the car."

"So have I. Honey, listen." Georgia explained everything. About running out of money, about having to leave the studio apartment, and about Aunt Norma's gift of a cottage. "You can meet me in Blackbird Beach if you want. The cottage is small, but I remember it as having two bedrooms."

Hopefully, that was still true. "Of course, I also have no idea what shape it's in, but I'm sure we can make it work."

"Oh mom, that would be great. I don't care if I have to sleep on a couch on the porch, anything is better than staying here with this cheater." She sobbed loudly. "I hate him."

Georgia nodded even though her daughter couldn't see that. "I'm so sorry, honey. I'll text you the address. We'll get through this, you'll see."

"Thanks, Mom. I love you." She got sniffly again.

"I love you, too. See you soon. And please drive safely."

"I will. Bye."

"Bye." Georgia hung up. She sighed. She'd thought Brendan was a nice guy. He'd seemed to really dote on Mia, but then Georgia had been wrong about Robert, too. And if she'd been wrong about her own husband, was she really that great a judge of character?

Apparently not.

She texted Mia the address of the cottage, then started the engine and headed out. Life had to get better, right?

It did, a little, in that her Pathfinder made it to Blackbird Beach without breaking down or spewing smoke from the engine. Georgia hadn't dared go faster than the speed limit, but she wasn't in a rush anyway.

Once she saw the sign welcoming her to town, she pulled over and fired up her GPS. She hadn't been to her aunt's cottage in so long she didn't trust herself to get there by memory alone. She knew it was by the beach, but that was about it.

With her navigation set up, she got back to driving. More slowly now, as it was dark and in a town like Blackbird Beach, there weren't all the big flashy hotels and souvenir shops to light things up.

There was no moon either, and as if nature wanted to remind Georgia of how crappy her life was, rain started coming down.

Thankfully, not in sheets, but enough to make seeing beyond her headlights tricky. She slowed down even more. If a car came up behind her, they'd just have to go around. She didn't want to miss her turn. She puttered along, peering closely at every new road.

At last, the GPS announced her turn and the street sign for Sea Glass Lane came into view.

The GPS took her directly to the cottage. As best as she could tell, it looked to be in decent shape. A second later, a flash of lightning helped her see better. Okay, maybe better than decent shape but outsides could be deceiving. Also that had been a split-second glimpse.

Although the cottage definitely looked smaller than she remembered, but then she'd been a kid when she'd been here last. Didn't matter. It was a roof over her head. And Mia's. Something they both desperately needed right now.

She leaned closer to the windshield and looked up at the sky. The rain didn't seem to be easing up. There was no way she was unloading the car in this. She glanced around for the most important things. A weekender bag with a couple changes of clothes and toiletries to get her through the night and the cooler with her perishables. There had to be something in there she could turn into dinner. Her stomach was growling, and she couldn't afford to order delivery.

Everything else could wait until the morning.

She turned the car off, plunging the property into darkness as the headlights went out. Maybe she'd get lucky and lightning would strike again so she could find her way. Just not too close. The way things had been going for her lately, she had to be careful what she wished for.

She hoisted the straps of the weekender over one shoulder and the straps of her purse over the other, then with cottage keys in hand, the package of stuff from the attorney under her arm, she opened the car door, grabbed the cooler, and made a run for it.

She was still sufficiently soaked by the time she reached the front porch. Such was her life and her luck. There'd been no lightning strike, either, but then again, maybe that was a good thing. It might have hit her.

She put the cooler down and started trying keys. How on earth could Aunt Norma need so many keys for one cottage? Was there a garage in the back? No, there couldn't be. There was nothing behind the house but a deck and the ocean. If the deck remained.

The ocean had to still be there, though. Didn't it? She listened, just to reassure herself, but it was impossible to hear anything over the rumbling thunder and pouring rain.

The fifth key turned the lock.

She exhaled in relief, pushed the door open and hauled her stuff inside. She felt around on the wall for a light switch. Took her a minute, but finally she found one. She flipped it on.

"Wow." The cottage was very pretty on the inside. Completely redone from what she remembered. Comfortable, but also very cute. And definitely current. It had that white-washed furniture and shabby coastal look so popular on all the decorating shows.

It didn't look like Aunt Norma's style, but people's tastes changed. Still, not a single antique or curious object. That seemed odd. Aunt Norma had always loved the interesting and unusual.

"Nice job, Aunt Norma. May you rest in peace," Georgia smiled, but sadness mixed with her gratefulness. "And thank you for your generous gift. You have no idea how much I needed this."

Or maybe Aunt Norma had known. Somehow. She'd always been a big one for intuition and trusting your gut.

Whatever Aunt Norma's reason for leaving Georgia the cottage, Georgia would never forget the thoughtful and timely gesture.

She took her cooler into the kitchen and opened the fridge to make sure it was cold and working. It was, although it was empty. Had Aunt Norma spent her last remaining time in a home? Because the place didn't look that lived in.

Or maybe the cottage had just had a thorough cleaning since Norma had passed.

Georgia emptied the cooler into the fridge, then took a little walk through the cottage, turning on lights and inspecting the rest of the place.

All of it was the same, very neat and cute and exactly like what you'd want a beach cottage to be.

The first bedroom had a beautiful iron bed in it. The second had two twins. Each bedroom had its own small bathroom.

The cottage was simple. An eat-in kitchen, a decent-sized living room, two bedrooms and two bathrooms. Plenty of space, really. And it was infinitely nicer than the studio apartment Georgia had been living in.

On a whim, she went to the sliding doors off the living room and peeked through to see if the ocean was visible. It wasn't. Nothing to see but rain. And the deck, which was thankfully still there. Looked like it had been redone since she'd last been here, too.

It was big and welcoming and on one side, boasted two handsome Adirondack chairs that faced the sea. On the other side, under a slated roof, sat a dining table with six chairs. There was a grill as well.

Strings of lights hung over the entire deck. They danced in the wind, but she could imagine the deck in nicer weather, the lights casting a warm glow over it all.

For the first time in a long time, Georgia smiled. She could just see herself and Mia out there having dinner. Sharing a bottle of wine.

Better times were ahead, she could feel it.

Then movement caught her eye. Something under the table. Another flash of lightning showed her exactly what. A big orange cat. He looked wet and miserable.

Poor thing. Georgia opened the slider. "Here kitty kitty. Come on, I won't hurt you."

He meowed at her and took a few steps forward but didn't leave the shelter of the table.

"Come on, you big lug. You can get dry in here." She stepped away from the open door.

A second later, he darted through.

She smiled, even though he'd left little wet paw prints on the hardwood floor. She closed the slider and went after him. He was sitting in the kitchen, licking his foot and looking very much like he'd just had a shower.

She grabbed a kitchen towel. "Do you mind if I dry you off a bit?"

He kept licking his foot.

She carefully reached out and scratched his damp head. He leaned into her hand and purred. "I guess we're friends, then, huh?"

That's when she realized he was wearing a collar with a tag. She held it toward the light. "Clyde. 12 Sea Glass Lane."

The cottage was 10 Sea Glass Lane, so he belonged to whoever lived next door. She hadn't seen a house beside this one, but with the rain and the darkness and her fixation on finding the cottage, that wasn't so surprising. She also hadn't been looking for one as the lot next door had always been empty when she was a child.

She turned the tag over. No phone number.

"Well, Clyde, if it stops raining, I'll let you back out but I'm not taking you home in this weather. You're just going to have to bunk here. I hope you can hold it until morning because I don't have a litter box, either." She started wiping him down with the towel, which he didn't seem to mind.

She looked around for something she might be able to use as a litter box. Even a small box with some shredded newspaper would work all right for a temporary solution.

Headlights shined in the front windows and a car honked outside. Clyde jumped down. Georgia put the towel on the counter and went to see if it was Mia, although she couldn't imagine who else it might be.

But of course it was, and Mia was already hurrying up the path with a suitcase, a tote bag, and her purse.

Georgia opened the door. "Welcome home, kiddo."

Chapter Two

Tired, heartsick, and now wet, Mia dropped the handle of her suitcase to wipe her eyes. That's when she finally got a good look at her mom. "Wow. You look…"

"Terrible?" Her mom laughed but there wasn't much joy in the sound.

"No, I was going to say great. I realize I haven't seen you in a couple months, but we've talked almost every day and you never said anything about being on a diet. Or working out. Or whatever you've been doing."

Georgia looked down at herself. "I haven't done anything."

"You look like you've lost twenty pounds. Maybe more."

"That's probably from stress. I guess my clothes have been getting a little looser."

Mia smiled as best she could with her heart breaking. She'd been so wrapped up in her own relationship and impending wedding that she'd lost track of her mom a little. "The divorce has been that hard, huh?"

"Kiddo, you don't know the half of it. Mainly because I haven't wanted to worry you, but yes, it's been very difficult. Now come in out of the weather and let's get you settled. You have enough on your plate without worrying about me. How was the drive?"

"It was fine. Rainy, but okay." Mia grabbed her suitcase and wheeled it in, then closed the door behind her and took a good look around. "Um, mom?"

"Yes?"

Mia pointed at the kitchen table where a large orange beast had just jumped up and was now perched, staring back at her. "When did you get a cat?"

Georgia looked in the same direction Mia was. "Ten minutes ago, but he's just a visitor. That's Clyde. He lives next door apparently, but I'm not taking him home in this weather so I'm letting him hang out here until it passes. Although we don't have a litter box for him so I'm not sure what to do about that."

"I see."

"Any chance you have a cardboard box and some newspapers we can shred to put in it in your car?"

"I actually have both of those. The box has some more of my clothes in it and the papers were already in there to be recycled. I'll run out and get them." Mia wiggled her fingers at him. "Hi, Clyde. I'm about to go back out in the rain for you. I hope you appreciate it."

Clyde chirped back at her with the sweetest tone.

Mia snorted. "And just like that, he's officially the nicest male I've interacted with in the last twenty-four hours." Tears threatened again as a wave of emotion brought them close to the surface.

"You want to talk about it?"

She tipped her head back and willed them away. "No. I'm done crying. For tonight anyway. I just want to forget what a mess my life is until tomorrow morning. Maybe longer."

"Okay. I understand."

"Thanks, Mom." It was so good to be with her mother. With someone who loved and supported her unconditionally. "I'll go get that stuff out of the car and be right back."

She grabbed her keys, dashed outside, grabbed the box and the papers and ran back in. "Here you go."

"Thank you. I'll take care of that in a few minutes." Georgia picked up Mia's tote bag. "First let's get you to your room. I hope you don't mind a twin bed."

"I'd sleep on the floor if I had to." She followed her mom through the living room. "Hey, this place is nice. Small, but I kind of like that. It's cozy."

"It is. I had no idea Aunt Norma had done so much with it." Georgia went through a door and turned on a light. "Here you go. To use your word, it's cozy, but you have your own bathroom. Both bedrooms do."

Mia put her purse on one of the beds. It was a postage stamp compared to the big fancy townhouse she'd shared with Brendan, but the cottage felt very different. In a good way. Warm. Welcoming. Safe. "It's a palace."

She sat down next to her purse and exhaled hard. The weight on her shoulders had lightened a little now that she was here with her mom. "I wish we had a bottle of wine."

Georgia smiled. "I have half a bottle. And it's nothing fancy. Screw top. Just the stuff that was on sale."

"White or red?" Mia held up her hands. "You know what, it doesn't matter."

They both laughed.

Her mom headed back out. "Let's see if we can find some glasses in the kitchen."

They found a whole set in the cabinet next to the fridge. Georgia got the wine out, emptied it into the two glasses and they took their drinks into the living room.

Mia took the couch, her mom took the matching chair. Clyde joined them, finding a spot on the rug in front of the television. "Have you talked to dad?"

Georgia shook her head. "We only communicate through lawyers these days. Well, through his attorney. I can't afford to communicate through mine. Have you talked to your father?"

"After what he did to you? No way. He's as dead to me as Brendan is. And Sarah for that matter." Mia sipped her wine. It wasn't bad for the cheap stuff, but that might have been need talking. "What happened to Aunt Norma?"

"I don't really know. I'll have to call the lawyer back tomorrow. He wanted to talk tonight but..." She shook her head.

"But what?"

"I only had a few short hours left to get out of that studio apartment with my stuff or the landlord would have changed the locks on me."

Mia sat up. "Mom, how did things get so bad?"

"Paying attorney's bills. Your father hiding money. My lack of useful skills making it impossible to get a decent job. I was making a little money doing some baking, but the studio kitchen was too small to keep that up." Georgia looked off into the distance. "I'm glad you went to college. You have something to fall back on."

Mia snorted. "Sure, hotel restaurant management is a hot market but only if you have experience and I've been waiting tables trying to work my way up for the last couple years." She sighed. "Brendan kept telling me it would all be different after we were married, and he'd made partner at the architectural firm."

She rubbed her forehead. "I can't believe he was sleeping with Sarah. My best friend! Former best friend. Who does that? Either of them. But as far as Brendan goes, he's a total creep and he can have Sarah, especially now that I know what a backstabbing homewrecker she is."

"I'm so sorry, honey. There really aren't enough words to describe how awful that is."

"Thanks, mom." Mia knew her mom understood. Mia's father had been a cheater, too. "I guess we both have less than stellar taste in men, huh?"

"At least I got you and your brother out of the deal. And you're getting away from Brendan before things got more complicated."

"True. Breaking up is easier than getting divorced." She looked at the fat diamond ring on her hand. "I keep forgetting I still have this on."

"Have you talked to Griffin lately?"

At her brother's name, Mia looked up. "No. You?"

"No. I left him a voicemail a couple days ago because I hadn't heard from him in a while, but he never called back. I should have told him I was moving. I just figured he'd call."

"Are you worried about him?"

Georgia shrugged. "Yes, but that's just what a mother does. He's an adult, though, so he should be able to take care of himself."

"Maybe he's on a shoot somewhere that has bad reception," Mia said. Griffin was doing his best to build a business as a photographer, which meant he was taking every job he could find. Regardless of how easy or difficult it was. And how little it paid.

"Maybe."

Mia's phone, tucked under her leg, vibrated with an incoming call. She picked it up and checked the screen, frowning as Brendan's name showed on the caller ID. She tapped the button to ignore. "Brendan. Like I'm interested in talking to him."

"Do you think you will?" Georgia sipped her wine. "At some point, I mean."

Mia sighed. "Maybe. But not about getting back together. Once a cheater—"

"Always a cheater," her mom finished.

The rain was still coming down outside. It was soothing in a way. Especially if Mia imagined it could wash Brendan out of her life and help her start over. "I guess I'll have to start looking for a job tomorrow. That is…if you're willing to let me stay here."

"Honey, you can stay as long as you'd like. It would be great to have you around. And we can share the bills. Can't be too much in a place this size. And at least we won't have rent."

"That'll help a lot." Mia raised her glass. "To new beginnings."

Georgia raised hers. "And to Aunt Norma's generosity. And perfect timing. May she rest in peace."

They both drank, then Mia watched the wine slide down the sides of the glass. "Why do you think she left the cottage to you and not to Aunt Lilly? She is the oldest."

"You mean besides the obvious reasons?" Georgia laughed. Then sighed. "To be honest, I don't know, except that my sister thinks she's better than all of us. At least I think she still does. I haven't talked to her in quite a few years. And even then, it wasn't much of a conversation."

Mia understood. Aunt Lilly was that person who'd already done everything and done it better than you.

She was stunningly beautiful and had used that beauty to marry a very wealthy man. She now spent her time going out to lunch with her wealthy friends. Or redecorating one of her many houses. Technically, redecorating was what she did for a living, but Mia didn't know if only redecorating your own homes counted as a business.

Every birthday, Mia got a card, a check for twenty-five dollars, and a scribbled note updating Mia on her aunt's life. Mia imagined Griffin got the same.

As of Mia's last birthday, Aunt Lilly had just had a custom shoe closet built in the Madrid property to house her designer shoes.

Mia had given serious consideration to sending the check back. "Did you tell her about you and dad?"

"No." Georgia grimaced. "She'd only say I told you so."

"Did she? Warn you about dad, I mean?"

Georgia huffed out a breath. "No. But she sure complained about everything at the wedding. The bridesmaid

23

dresses were the wrong color for her, the flowers were skimpy, the hall was impersonal, the food was cold, the—well, you get the idea."

"I do." Mia nodded. "She's always been nice enough to Griff and me. I mean, nice is relative, I suppose."

"At least she remembers you on your birthdays. For that I'm grateful."

"Mom," Mia said. "A twenty-five-dollar check isn't breaking her bank."

"No, but it's the thought that counts, right?"

"I guess. Honestly, I'm not sure why she bothers."

"Maybe…because she could never have kids of her own."

Mia thought about that. "Maybe that's why she resented you."

Georgia stared into her wine. "That's not the only reason."

Mia sat up a little straighter. Was her mom about to reveal the real reason she and her sister had such a contentious relationship? "What else was there?"

Georgia opened her mouth, then closed it again and shook her head. "It's late and that's a long story and I'm tired. I need to fix up that litter box for Clyde, then I'm going to take a shower and go to bed."

"Okay. Me, too." But Mia wasn't about to let that story remain untold for long.

Gulf Coast Cottage

Chapter Three

Clyde slept curled up on the end of Georgia's bed until nearly six a.m., when she woke up to find him sitting next to her, staring at her in the dark. She could just make him out by the glow of the clock's blue LED numbers.

As soon as she sighed at him, he meowed at her.

"If you're hungry, I hate to tell you this, but we don't have any breakfast for you. Or maybe you just want to go back out so you can go home? Come on." She got up and padded barefoot to the sliders, trying to make as little noise as possible so as not to wake Mia. She opened them enough for Clyde to slip out.

He did too, trotting off into the dark like he had a destination in mind.

Georgia stood there a moment. The rain had stopped, and the sea lent a salty tang to the air that made her spirit feel alive for the first time in months. What a glorious spot this was. And with the beach only steps away.

The waves crashed softly in the distance and she smiled. Such an amazing gift her aunt had given her. Not just this cottage, but the chance to start over. She owed Norma a debt she could never repay.

After another few moments, she closed the sliders and went back to her bedroom, but this time she cracked her window enough to hear the waves.

She fell asleep again with nature's lullaby the only white noise she needed.

"Mom. Mom? Are you up?"

Georgia blinked and looked at the bedside clock. "I am now." Almost eight. Not too terrible a wake-up time considering stress and worry usually woke her up long before then. If she slept at all. "What's wrong? Did something happen?"

"Nothing's wrong, but holy cow, you should see the house next door. Did you know Aunt Norma lived next to a mansion?"

Georgia rubbed her eyes. "A mansion?" Mia had to be exaggerating. Blackbird Beach had rules that prevented anyone from building anything too big. Well, big was probably okay. Tall was not.

"Seriously, it's amazing. I mean, it could use some paint and yard work to start with, but it's still gorgeous. Great bones, as they say."

Georgia got up, pulled her robe on over her nightgown, and went out to the living room. Mia was standing at the windows, peering out.

Georgia joined her. The house on the next lot over was definitely a mansion. Easily three stories, which had to be a violation of the Blackbird Beach building codes. "How about that. How on earth did they get that thing built with the restrictions in this town?"

"Somebody knew somebody. Or somebody had money."

"Or both," Georgia said. She looked at Mia. "Hungry?"

"Starving. I never really had dinner last night."

"Neither did I."

Mia yawned. "And if I don't get some coffee I'll die."

Georgia thought about the meager groceries she'd brought with her. Most of what had been in her cooler had been condiments. "I think I have enough to make pancakes and probably two pots of coffee, but that's about it. At some point, I'll have to go shopping today or lunch will be saltines and peanut butter. Or canned peaches and tuna. I suppose Clyde would like that."

Mia laughed. "I can do the shopping. I have my tip money from the week. Which reminds me, I need to call Bella Luna's and tell them I'm not going to be in for a while. Or ever, I suppose."

Bella Luna's was the Italian restaurant where Mia had been employed. "You do that, and I'll get to work on coffee and breakfast."

"No one will be there, it's too early, but I can leave them a message. Then I'm going to shower. But I'll be quick."

"Take your time. The first batch of pancakes is just for practice anyway."

Mia gave her mom an impromptu hug. "Thanks for letting me stay with you."

"Kiddo, even if all I had was a tent on the beach, I'd make room for you."

"Thanks." With a big smile, Mia went off to get ready.

Georgia smiled as she watched her daughter. Truth was, she loved having Mia around. It certainly made things less lonely. And now that they were both in a similar spot in life, they could help each other out.

It was a perfect situation, really. And much better than going through it alone.

Georgia went into the kitchen. There was already a coffee pot on the counter. She found filters in one of the cabinets, then dug around for a frying pan large enough for the pancakes. The cabinets were weirdly empty of all but the very basics, once again prompting Georgia to wonder if Aunt Norma's last days had been spent in a nursing home. Or some kind of hospice care, maybe?

If so, someone had to have been in here and cleaned things out. Who would have done that? A friend? The attorneys?

She sighed, remembering she had to call them back. Well, that wasn't such a bad thing. After all, the first call had brought her this cottage. What more could there be to do? Sign some paperwork? Maybe the answer was in the package they'd sent. She'd look it over after they'd eaten.

She got the coffee brewing, then found a bowl and made batter with the half box of mix she had. Thankfully, she also had the egg, milk and butter required. Not much of any of them, but enough to get their breakfast made. She added a little extra vanilla and a dash of cinnamon, too.

As she cooked, she thought about how things could be different now. About possibly starting up her baking business again. Would locals be interested?

Blackbird Beach didn't really have the tourist trade that other towns along the Gulf did, but a lot of that was because the town kept things so locked down. There were no big hotels. At least there hadn't been. And who'd want to come to a place that had so few places to stay?

Although the house next door made Georgia wonder if restrictions had loosened up lately.

Mia came out, dressed in cutoff denim shorts and a t-shirt with her long brown hair wrapped up in a towel. She sat at the small kitchen table with an old envelope and a pen. She flipped the envelope onto the blank side and held the pen poised to write. "Okay, let's make a grocery list."

Georgia shook her head, smiling.

"What?"

"If I dressed like that, someone would think I was trying too hard. You, however, look like a supermodel." Georgia laughed softly, amazed at how beautiful her daughter was. Brendan was an idiot. And Sarah was…not worth Mia's time.

"Mom, I do not look like a supermodel."

"Okay, I'll give you that. Most supermodels look like they need to eat a sandwich. You at least have some curves."

"Mom." But Mia was grinning all the same. "What do we need from the store? Wait. There is a store in town, right?"

"Yes, if I remember right it's called…Ludlows, I think. Of course, that was years ago. Might have been bought out by a big chain by now."

"I'll look it up on my GPS."

"Get eggs, milk for the coffee, some more butter. Oh, coffee, obviously. A loaf of bread and maybe some lunch meat for sandwiches. I have some peanut butter and jelly, so we can go that route too."

Mia was scribbling away. "How about for dinner?"

Georgia tried to think of the cheapest way to feed two people. "Are you sick of pasta from working at Bella Luna?"

"Nope. You want spaghetti?"

Georgia nodded. "Sure. And whatever sauce is on sale. If there's anything else on sale that looks like a good deal, that's fine too. I could roast a chicken if they're a good buy. Maybe with some carrots and a few potatoes. You know, anything like that. But don't go crazy. We can live simply for a while. At least until there's money coming in."

Mia looked over the list. "You forgot wine."

Georgia laughed. "True, but that's not exactly a budget item."

"Maybe not, but it is a necessity." Mia added it to the list. "Hey, I'll see if the grocery store is hiring. I could be a cashier."

Georgia sighed. "You could be. But you're a little overqualified."

"Mom, a job is a job. And we need money."

"I know. I was thinking I might do a little job hunting myself today."

The coffee pot sputtered, signaling the brew was done.

Mia hopped up to fix herself a cup. She opened a few cabinets before she found the mugs. "Huh. Aunt Norma didn't really have a lot of stuff, did she?"

"I think she might have been in a nursing home for a while. Someone must have come in and cleaned everything out. Maybe the attorneys she hired. I'm going to ask them since I have to call them today anyway. I hope her things weren't just taken to a thrift shop or sold off. It would be nice to have something of hers to remember her by."

Gulf Coast Cottage

Mia poured two cups of coffee, putting sugar and milk into hers. "It's weird that they didn't leave anything personal. No pictures or anything."

Georgia nodded as she put pancakes onto two plates. "I noticed. It is odd. But then, maybe there was some kind of estate sale? Or her things were put into storage? I have no idea. Hopefully, the attorneys will tell me."

She carried the plates to the table and Mia brought the coffee along with some silverware.

Mia put the mugs down. "Is there any syrup?"

"Oh. Yes. But it's still in the car. In a box marked kitchen."

"I'll get it. Where in the car?"

"Back seat on the passenger's side. Keys are right there on the counter."

Mia picked them. "Be right back. Gotta have syrup."

She left, giving Georgia a chance to once again wonder how Brendan could be so stupid. Mia was a bright, beautiful girl with a kind heart.

Mia came back in, box in her arms. "It is so pretty outside. I am definitely taking a walk on the beach at some point today. In fact, I want to do it every day."

"That's a great idea."

Mia opened the box and rummaged around for the syrup, then brought it to the table. "Thanks for breakfast. I'll make dinner. Italian is kind of my specialty."

Georgia laughed. "Okay."

Amazing how much things could improve in less than twenty-four hours. Sure, they didn't have much money, but they had each other. And a place to stay. Whatever came their way, they'd get through it.

31

And Georgia definitely had a feeling *something* was coming their way.

Chapter Four

Mia unpacked her car, putting the clothes on the bed and the rest of the boxes and bags in a pile on the floor of her room to deal with later. Right now, she just couldn't. She put on a little makeup and dried her hair before heading out to get groceries. Her mom's list had been pretty sparse, but Mia understood her mother was trying not to spend too much money.

Well, they had to eat. And Mia had a decent amount saved up from working. Not that she was going to spend it all on steaks and lobster, but she was going to do her best to stock the kitchen with enough to see them through the week.

They should be able to find work by then. She hoped.

She drove carefully, minding her GPS but also trying to get a feel for the town. It was really cute. Lots of mom-and-pop stores, including a bookstore, a beauty shop, a little diner, and a secondhand store that was run by the Methodist church.

Mia wondered if that's where Aunt Norma's things had ended up. She also wondered if the diner was hiring. Waitressing was definitely something she could do.

The grocery store was still called Ludlows, just like her mom had said. Mia parked, grabbed one of her reusable bags that she always kept in the car, and headed in, but not before taking a quick look around. Across the street was a florist, then the office for the local newspaper, the Blackbird Gazette. Then the thrift shop, Bon Voyage Vintage.

As far as Mia was concerned, every single business in town might be hiring and was worth investigating. Which she would. After she took her groceries home and put on something more professional than cutoffs and a Wonder Woman t-shirt.

She grabbed a cart on her way in and headed straight to produce for some fresh fruit and veggies. Eating cheaply didn't mean skimping on healthy food. Although she hoped there would be a few things on sale. Deep sales.

A cute guy in a blue Ludlows apron was restocking bananas. And they were on sale. Mia picked up a small bunch.

"Morning. Welcome to Ludlows."

She glanced at him. Very cute. Cuter than Brendan anyway. But then roadkill was cuter than Brendan right now. "Thanks."

"Anything I can help you with, just let me know."

"I will." His name tag said Lucas. He seemed nice. That and her need for gainful employment suddenly got the best of her. "I'm Mia. I'm new in town. Any chance Ludlows is hiring?"

Lucas smiled, showing off dimples in his cheeks that weakened her knees ever so slightly. He was actually a lot cuter than Brendan. "Not that I know of, but I'd be happy to take your application."

"Oh."

"Hey, there might be some part time hours available. I can ask my dad."

"Your dad works here?"

"My dad owns the store. I'm Lucas Ludlow. Assistant manager. And produce manager." He laughed. "That's what happens when you work for your family. You get to do more than one job."

She stuck her hand out. "Nice to meet you, Lucas. I'm Mia. Which I already told you. Mia Carpenter."

"Nice to meet you, too." He shook her hand and the warmth of his skin reminded her of Brendan and his cold betrayal. How on earth had she not seen him for what he was sooner?

Lucas added some more bananas to the display. "Did you say you just moved into the area?"

Mia nodded, happy to distract herself with small talk. "Yep. Last night, actually."

"Well, we should get you a Ludlows loyalty card. In fact, it's good for ten percent off your bill the day you sign up." He leaned in like he was about to share a secret. "That even includes beer and wine."

It was as if a choir of angels had just started singing. "Well, then I definitely need one. That's a great deal. And our place is empty."

"Our place?"

Had he just glanced at her hand? Was he looking for a ring? She was suddenly glad she'd left hers on the nightstand. "My mom and I are sharing a place. A cottage on the beach. We're kind of, uh, starting over."

"Blackbird Beach is a great place to do that."

"That's nice to hear."

"Come on," he said. "Let's get you that loyalty card and an application."

She followed him to the customer service desk. Ludlows seemed pretty well stocked for a smaller store. So far, the prices seemed good too. Maybe that was how they competed with the big guys.

She filled out the forms, taking a little longer with the application. Finally she finished them and handed the two sheets of paper to Lucas. "I didn't intend to go job hunting dressed like this."

He took the papers, handed her back a loyalty card, and shrugged. "It's Florida. Everyone's dressed like that." His smile got a little wider. "Of course, not everyone looks like you when they're dressed like that."

She laughed, feeling her cheeks heat just a little. "Thanks. And thanks for the help. I should get my shopping done. My mom will think I got lost."

"I'll see you around then."

"Maybe sooner if some hours open up."

He nodded, smiling. "Maybe sooner."

She wheeled her cart through the store with a light step. Her smile seemed stuck in place. It wasn't that she wanted to hop back into another relationship. But it was nice to know the possibility existed. Even nicer to know that a guy like Lucas seemed to be of the same mind.

Mia got her shopping done, buying a little more than she had planned due to her new loyalty card. Before long, her cart was almost full. All basics, really. And all aimed at budget minded dinners, although she did add a package of reasonably priced steaks, some nice cheese, and a small box of fancy crackers.

There was no reason not to take advantage of the one-time discount, especially since it included wine. She had six bottles in the cart. Maybe that was too many, but how often did a discount on vino come along? As for the groceries, she'd only splurged on a few things and she wasn't going to feel bad about that. A nice dinner would be fun.

They both deserved a nice dinner as far as Mia was concerned.

She didn't see Lucas again on her way out of the store and that left her wishing that she had. She'd looked for him, too. Maybe he was back in produce.

She loaded the groceries in her trunk, her mind full of thoughts. Had he been flirting with her? Or was that just wishful thinking? Did she want him to flirt with her? Really, she just wanted to be friends. At least initially. But what would it be like to work in the same store as him?

She hoped it would be okay. It would have to be. Because even if all they could offer her was part time, she was going to take it. A job was a job, and she needed the money. Getting to work next to Lucas would just be a bonus she hadn't anticipated.

"Mia, there you are."

She was just about to shut her trunk when she looked up to see Lucas headed toward her. "Did I forget something?"

"No, I just talked to my dad and he said we could absolutely use some part time cashier help. I know this is short notice, but could you come back today for a few hours of training and to do the new hire paperwork?"

"Absolutely. Can you give me an hour to get these groceries home and get changed?"

"Sure, take your time. Do you have khaki pants? We'll give you a Ludlows shirt."

"Khaki pants are no problem." Her time waitressing had made that an easy answer.

"We'll see you soon, then."

She nodded. "Absolutely. And thank you."

Her smile stayed with her all the way back to the cottage.

Chapter Five

Georgia got to work on the dishes as soon as Mia left. She didn't mind making breakfast and cleaning up, not when Mia was getting groceries and paying for them.

That filled Georgia with a mix of emotions. On one hand, it hurt her that she didn't have the money to do that for them. On the other, it filled her with pride that her daughter had stepped up so generously.

Georgia was wrist-deep in hot, soapy water when someone knocked at the door. Couldn't be Mia, she'd only been gone twenty minutes. "Just a second!"

She grabbed a dish towel, wiped her hands, and went to the door. When she opened it, she found a stranger on the other side. A man slightly older than her and wearing a very nice business suit. Good shoes too. Not a look you saw every day in a seaside Florida town. He was also carrying a briefcase. She couldn't imagine who he was or what he wanted, but she was instantly wary. "Can I help you?"

"Are you Georgia Carpenter?"

"I am." If her ex had sent someone... But why? "Who are you?" There was a time to be polite and a time to be straightforward. The straightforward time seemed like now.

"I'm Roger Gillum. We spoke last night." He hesitated like he was waiting to see if she remembered.

"You're the attorney."

"Yes, ma'am."

"And you drove all the way out here?" Her wariness hadn't eased up. "Whatever you need to tell me must be important."

"It is. Also, it wasn't that far of a drive as my office is here in Blackbird Beach. And I thought it best to come by since you weren't answering your phone."

"I'm not? Oh! I probably forgot to put it on the charger last night and left it on silent. Sorry about that." Suddenly she remembered her manners and stepped out of the way. After all, this man had basically kept her from sleeping in her car last night. Mia too. "Come in, please."

"Thank you." He wiped his feet, making her like him a little more than she already did.

"Is this about the papers in the package you sent me?"

"Yes. We need to get them signed and notarized soon so that we can have the deeds transferred into your name."

"Okay, I can probably get that done today. Wait. You said deeds. With an S."

"That's correct. One for each property."

Georgia stood very still as she thought back. But all she could remember was her aunt owning this cottage, nothing more. "How many properties are there?"

"These two cottages and the house between."

Her hand moved slowly to point at the palace next door. "It sounds like you're talking about the place over there, but that can't be possible."

He blinked, eyes narrowing like he didn't quite understand why his words weren't making sense. "Why can't it be?"

"Because the house next door is enormous. There's no way my great aunt could have bought that place. Also, I'm pretty sure that house is in code violation, unless the building laws have changed in Blackbird Beach."

"They haven't. And she didn't buy it, she had it built. She got the money when her third husband passed away. He was quite wealthy."

"Third husband?" That was news to Georgia. "I don't remember there being a third husband. That seems like the kind of thing that wouldn't have slipped my mind."

"She didn't tell anyone about him because, in her words, she didn't think anyone would understand their age difference."

Georgia hadn't had enough coffee for this conversation. "Would you like a cup of coffee and to go have a seat in the living room? I feel like coffee and sitting down are required for me to fully understand all this."

He nodding, cracking a little smile. "Coffee would be lovely, thank you."

"I'll get it and be right in. Milk and sugar?"

"Yes, please. Just a touch of both." He went into the living room.

She stared at the coffee pot, glad there was half a pot left and that it was still hot. His words hadn't sunk in and she wasn't sure they would. Three properties.

As exciting as that was, not to mention unbelievable, how on earth was she going to afford all of that? Owning property meant upkeep, and taxes, water and electric bills, insurance.

All of those things and more she was probably forgetting. On top of that, she couldn't think of a job that would pay her enough to afford all of those items.

She fixed two cups of coffee, thankful she had plenty of sugar left over from her baking venture and took them into the living room.

He'd taken the chair, leaving the couch or loveseat for her. She put his coffee down in front of him.

"Thank you."

"You're welcome." She sat, sipping hers despite how hot it was. She needed to be as alert as possible. "All right. She had a third husband who was younger than her?"

"Older. Cecil Barnesworth. She was sixty-eight when they married. He was ninety-two."

Georgia's brows went up. "I see. But if she loved him, what did age matter? Although…"

"Yes?" Roger waited.

"My sister, Lilly, definitely would have had something to say." Boy, would she ever. Although Lilly had married a very wealthy man so maybe she wouldn't? Hard to say with Lilly. "I can understand Aunt Norma wanting to keep things to herself. It was her business anyway. So Cecil left her a lot of money?"

"He did and not long after they were married. In fact, he expired two weeks after they returned from their honeymoon cruise around the world."

Georgia's eyebrows went slightly higher. "That sounds amazing. The cruise, I mean. Not him dying right after. Wow. How devastating for her." Poor Aunt Norma. Widowed so soon after being married.

Roger smiled. "I knew what you meant. He left her everything, which was quite a substantial sum. But she was heartbroken. He'd already bought the land beside this cottage, so she built herself the home they'd planned on."

"That's a wonderful story. Sad, but sweet too. Still, I have to ask, how did she ever get the approval to build a house that big?"

Roger cleared his throat, then occupied himself with his coffee.

Did he not want to tell her? "I promise, nothing you can say about my great aunt will surprise me. Not after hearing about the third uncle I never knew."

He put his cup down. "I suppose that's true. Well, I don't know this for certain, but rumor has it she was...very *close* with one of the town council members and he got her an exemption for that third floor."

Georgia tipped her head. "Very close?"

"Intimately close." He sighed. "All I know is based on rumors and I hate to speak ill of the dead. Your aunt never told anyone the real story. Not to my knowledge, anyway."

Things suddenly became clear for Georgia. "I don't think it's speaking ill to say she used her feminine wiles to get what she wanted. If that's what happened. Which is what it sounds like." Georgia had no doubt that was exactly what had happened. Aunt Norma had always had a way with men that defied logic.

"If it helps, she also made a generous donation to the Blackbird Beach library. It's because of her they managed to stay open, actually."

"That's really nice to hear." Georgia laughed. "Maybe that balances out whatever she did for the exemption."

"I'm sure in her mind, it was an even exchange. Anyway, you are her sole heir."

"Which is amazing because I'm not her only heir. But she always was kind of a magical, bigger than life person to me. When I was a kid, coming to visit her here in this cottage was one of the best things ever." Georgia smiled, then reality set in. "I feel terrible I didn't get to see her one last time."

"About that." He opened up his briefcase and took out a slim ceramic jar. "It was her desire that her ashes remain in her house. Which is now your house."

"I can take care of that. Except…I have to be honest with you, Mr. Gillum. I don't have a clue how I can afford three properties. Especially when one of them is that behemoth next door. Look at it. At best it needs to be painted and have some yard work done. At worst, well, I have no idea what the inside looks like, but I bet there's maintenance to be done. A lot of it."

She took a breath. "On top of that, I don't have a job, I'm going through the most vicious divorce you can imagine, and my daughter had to move in with me because she just found out her fiancé has been cheating on her. We aren't exactly financially flush right now."

He smiled, which wasn't the reaction she'd been expecting. "Norma didn't just leave you the properties. She left you her entire estate. That includes the accounts. Mrs. Carpenter, money is not going to be a problem for you."

He took a large, thick envelope out of his briefcase and laid it on the table. "Most of what you need to know is in here."

Georgia's mouth was open, but she didn't quite have the energy to close it just yet.

Mr. Gillum pulled out some more paperwork from his briefcase. "Sadly, the main house definitely does need some work done, so I don't expect the money to last you forever, but it should be enough to keep you on your feet for a bit. Long enough to get the inn back up and running anyway. Or sell it, if that's what you decide to do."

"The inn?"

He nodded. "Before your aunt took ill, she ran the house as the Sea Glass Inn. Did very well with it, too. There aren't many places to stay in this town. But the older she got and the sicker she became, the harder it was to manage and well, at a certain point, she shut it all down. You can see the result. The two side cottages were the only things she kept going since their maintenance didn't cause her any bother."

Georgia looked around. That explained why there were no personal possessions or photos and no food in the kitchen. This wasn't where Aunt Norma had lived. This was a rental.

When she looked at Mr. Gillum again, he was laying a pen across the paperwork he'd taken out. "I just need you to sign in a few places."

"Before I do that, I need to know one thing, Mr. Gillum."

"I'll be happy to answer if I can."

"Is there any way my soon to be ex-husband would be able to get his hands on any of this? Because that would be more than I could bear."

Mr. Gillum smiled. "I'll make sure that doesn't happen. Norma asked me to help you in whatever way you needed. I told her I would."

Georgia picked up the pen.

Chapter Six

Mia walked in, hands loaded down with grocery bags, ready to tell her mom about the job at Ludlows. But she found her mother waiting in the kitchen and practically vibrating with excitement. Mia put the bags on the table, then turned to her mom. "All right, something's going on. What happened? Did you finally get a hold of Griff?"

"No, but I am definitely going to need to call him. You are not going to believe this."

Mia crossed her arms. The rest of the groceries and the news about the part time work could wait a minute. "What is it? Spill it?"

Her mother's brows lifted, and her face held the kind of curious, playful joy Mia hadn't seen in a long time. "I found out who owns the house next door."

Mia's mind went wild. She squeezed her hands together in front of her and leaned forward. "Is it a celebrity? Please tell me it's Zac Efron. Please tell me it's Zac Efron and he's in the house right now."

Her mother rolled her eyes. "No, it's not owned by Zac Efron."

"Then who?"

Her mother's playful joy returned. "Me."

"Me what?"

"It's owned by me. *I* own it. Well, Great Aunt Norma did but it's part of what she left to me. This cottage, the big house next door, and the other little cottage on the side of that."

Mia stared at her mother as the words processed. "You can't be serious. Are you serious?" She reached out, found a kitchen chair and sat down. "That's, that's…unbelievable."

"I know." Georgia squealed softly. Not a sound Mia had ever heard come out of her mom before. Except maybe when Mia had told her about the engagement. "And it gets better."

"I don't know how that could be possible. Unless she also left you money."

Still making the squealing sound, Georgia started nodding.

"Holy smokes. Mom. There's money too?"

"There is." Georgia sat down. "I know. I'm as flabbergasted as you."

"I am really glad I bought some steaks. We definitely need a celebratory dinner tonight."

"Mia, steaks are expensive."

She shrugged, smiling. "Yeah, but I used my loyalty card. And I got a job."

"You did? Mia, that's great news. Where?"

"Ludlows. It's just part time. I'll be a cashier. But it's a start, right?"

"Totally. I'm so happy for you."

Mia laughed. "I think your news is a little more exciting."

"Oh, speaking of that, there's more."

Mia's mouth gaped open. "Please tell me Aunt Norma left us brand new cars."

"No," her mom said. "But that would be nice. My Pathfinder is on its last legs. Wheels. Whatever."

"Then what is it?"

"Aunt Norma used to run the house as an inn. The Sea Glass Inn, to be exact. The lawyer thinks the money she left me will be enough to get the place in order again and reopened." Georgia reached across the table and took her daughter's hand. "I'm going to need you, kiddo. You and that college degree. I don't know the first thing about running an inn."

Mia gasped. "Oh, mom. That would be amazing. I mean, I'm not the most experienced, as you know, but I will work so hard you won't believe it."

"I know you will, honey. I want you to be my partner in this. A new beginning, right? For both of us. Together."

Mia almost felt like crying. Happy tears, of course, but the emotion welling up in her was hard to contain. "Absolutely. A new beginning. I'm with you completely. Whatever you need me to do, I'll do it."

"Great." Georgia squeezed Mia's hand before letting it go. "Still, it's a good thing you got that part time job. I have no idea how long it's going to take to get the house in good enough shape for paying customers. You want to go over and have a look around with me? I can't imagine what all is in there. I mean, three floors! Oh, that reminds me, apparently Aunt Norma got a special allowance from the town council to build that third story because she was *very* friendly with one of the councilmen."

"What?" Mia laughed. "That's crazy."

"That's Aunt Norma."

"Well, I'd love to look at the house with you, but I can't. I told Lucas I'd come right back to take care of paperwork and do some training."

"Okay, no problem. I'll look at the other cottage while you're gone, but I'll wait to check out the house until you get back. Then we'll do it together. What do you think?"

"I think that's awesome. Thank you. I also think I really need to get the rest of the groceries out of the car."

My mom got up. "I'll help."

As they unpacked the car, then worked on unloading the bags, they talked about all the possibilities the inn could bring them. The chance at a new start was a gift, one Mia knew a lot of people would have loved to get.

She couldn't help but think they were blessed to have the opportunity.

And it felt good to know she was going to get to help her mom in a meaningful way.

Georgia came in with the wine, which the cashier at Ludlows had put into a box for easier carrying. "Mia, you bought too much. Food is one thing but six bottles of wine? This must have cost every bit of what you had."

"It didn't, I swear. I signed up for the Ludlows loyalty card and with that you get ten percent off on your first purchase. Seemed silly to waste that by not doing a big shop. Especially when it included wine."

"In that case maybe you didn't get enough." Georgia grinned. "Just teasing."

Mia laughed. "Trust me, I had that thought. Although I suppose you can go sign up for a loyalty card on the next visit and do the same thing."

"Good thinking. No reason we both shouldn't have one." She set the box on the table. "Are you going to change before you go back?"

"Oh! Thanks for reminding me. I have to find my khaki pants. They're going to give me a shirt. I really need to fix myself up a little better too."

"Go, I'll put the rest of this away. Getting started on the new job is more important."

"Thanks, mom." Mia went back to her room where the bulk of her things were still heaped in a pile.

She hoisted her suitcase onto the other bed and started digging through the mess. She'd been in such a hurry to leave that she'd shoved things into it willy nilly.

At last she found her khaki pants, which were a little wrinkled, and a nice short-sleeved blouse. Even if they were giving her a Ludlows shirt, it wouldn't hurt to go in looking better than she had the first time.

She braided her hair back, found some small hoop earrings and then added a little more makeup, playing up her eyes. Finally, she put on the watch that had been her college graduation present, then gave herself a quick check in the mirror. Everything seemed to be in order.

She went back out to see her mom who was organizing the cabinets now that they actually had food in them. "What do you think?"

"You look great. They're going to be very glad they hired you. In fact, I bet you get more hours before you know it."

"Thanks. Let's just hope I get the hang of the register."

Georgia smiled. "Honey, you're one of the smartest people I know. You'll have it in no time."

"Thanks, mom. I'll be home in a few hours, I think. Then we'll look at the house and after that, make steaks on the grill. A nice celebratory dinner. What do you think? Sound like a plan?"

Her mom nodded. "It does indeed."

Mia grabbed her keys and her purse, still on the kitchen table and headed out to Ludlows, ready to start the new chapter of her life.

And maybe just a little eager to see Lucas again.

Chapter Seven

Georgia finished setting up the kitchen, then changed into shorts and T-shirt. Granted, her shorts were longer than Mia's had been, and her T-shirt was a graceful scoop neck from Lands' End instead of an homage to Wonder Woman, but she felt cute. Good news had a way of lifting the spirit.

She brushed her hair into a ponytail, then covered her face, neck, and ears with her favorite tinted sunscreen. If living in Florida had taught her anything, it was the importance of protecting her skin. Especially now that she was getting older.

Someday, like if the inn made money, she'd love to be one of those women who got regular facials. And went to the salon instead of covering their gray with box dye. Thankfully, she was still a week or two away from reaching the desperate stage of root growth.

She put her sunglasses on, tucked her phone into her back pocket and managed to get the tangle of keys into her front one. That mass of keys made sense now that she understood it was for three properties.

It was also a little smaller since she'd been able to remove the keys for the cottage they were in. No sense in taking those. This was Blackbird Beach. No one locked their doors.

Although, habits died hard. She locked the front door before going out the sliders. She'd leave those unlocked. And she'd be back before Mia got home.

She went out onto the deck. The second cottage was too close to drive to and since she was walking, she was going to do it on the beach.

Clyde was lounging under the table again, but he wasn't all the way under. His back half was getting some good sun.

"Hey, buddy. I just realized something." She crouched down next to him, giving him a scratch on the head. "According to the address on your collar, you must have been my aunt's cat. I guess that makes you mine now, too. But who's been taking care of you? It's been months since she passed. Or are you just that good at roughing it?

Georgia ran her hand down his back. He certainly didn't feel like he'd missed any meals. He rolled over, showing her his belly and confirming that he was both fat and happy.

"Don't worry, Clyde, we'll take care of you. But I am going to call Mr. Gillum and make sure you really did belong to her. I'd hate to take you away from a family who already loves you."

He made a few air biscuits, then closed his eyes.

"Your concern is overwhelming." She laughed, then got up and went down to the beach, taking the meandering path between the dune grasses and other plants. There were even some morning glories with their happy blue blooms and some smaller yellow flowers in the mix.

She'd left her shoes behind and she was glad for it. The sand was soft and sugary and felt wonderful between her toes.

There was a gorgeous breeze, too. Even in early October, the weather was beautiful. She leaned into the breeze, closing her eyes and letting it wash over her. She inhaled the salt air and smiled, listening to the waves crash and the gulls cry. She opened her eyes and took in the amazing scene before her. Was this actually her life now? How had things gone from dark and desperate to bright and beautiful?

The hard work that lay ahead, and she knew there'd be plenty, was a small price to pay for this enormous reward.

Once again, she found herself wishing she could thank Aunt Norma in person. There had to be something Georgia could do. Some way she could memorialize her aunt. Hopefully, an idea would come to her.

She walked to the water's edge to where the sand was wet from the last wave. Shells of all kinds, some perfect, some broken, most no larger than a half dollar, dotted the sand. She didn't have far to go today, but she could see herself taking long walks on this beach. Maybe starting a little collection of shells in a big glass jar.

She hoped she had enough time to walk this beach every day. It would be a shame to live here and not take advantage of the opportunity.

Here and there, frosted bits of sea glass mixed with the shells. She picked up a pale green piece and tucked it in the pocket that didn't have keys.

Still smiling, she made her way along the water toward the second cottage but stopped for a few moments to look at the backside of the inn.

It definitely needed work. Painting for sure, since the once serene pale blue paint was peeling and chipping more than it was still attached. The white trim was dingy and chipped, too. There were railings that needed to be repaired, too. What she could see of the roof looked fine, but she was no expert.

One of the coach lights on the back porch was hanging loose and there was no furniture to speak of, but she could imagine the expansive deck with little seating areas and places for guests to sit and read, or have a glass of wine, or just watch the water.

All of the windows looked intact, but most of the curtains were closed. Georgia hoped that didn't mean the house wasn't well ventilated. Dampness could be a problem otherwise, and if there was mold, that would be a lot of money to deal with.

The landscaping, such as it was, was wild and weedy and would need a firm hand. Everything was either overgrown or dead. Maybe, if there was money, Georgia would see about adding a gazebo in the back yard. That might be nice for weddings. And weddings would be a good way to bring in more guests.

She almost laughed. Look at her, thinking like a businesswoman already. She knew she was getting ahead of herself, but maybe she could do this after all. She was certainly going to try. Mia's help would be invaluable.

As tempting as it was to walk around the outside, Georgia had promised Mia they'd explore together and taking a spin around the place alone felt like a minor violation of that promise.

So, instead of going closer, she continued on her way to the second cottage. The one she and Mia were in was pale yellow. This second one was nearly the same green as the sea glass in her pocket.

The trio of buildings would look picture-perfect once the inn was restored. Maybe she'd get a photo taken and have it turned into a postcard for guests to send. Or keep. That would be a fun thing to do. A little memento, a little advertising, maybe get some new business out of it.

The sand sank under her feet as she made her way inland. The cottage looked exactly like hers. Same back deck, same Adirondack chairs, same covered area with a table, same hanging lights.

She took a moment to brush the sand off her feet, then went to the back sliders and started trying her keys.

Took a few tries, but she finally got the right one. She slid the glass door open and stepped inside. The cottage looked more lived in than the one she was in. Maybe it hadn't been cleaned since the last renter. She walked through to the kitchen and frowned. There was still coffee in the coffee pot. And a dish in the sink.

"Can I help you?"

With a shriek, she turned around to find a very handsome man standing behind her. Wearing nothing but a pale blue towel wrapped around his waist. She made herself look at his face. He seemed to be about her age.

And in incredible shape.

"I...I..."

"Cat got your tongue?"

His teasing remark helped her senses come back to her. Georgia frowned at him. "Why are you naked in my cottage?"

His brows arched in obvious amusement. "Ma'am, I'm not naked. And this is not your cottage."

"It is so." She dangled the keys still in her hand. "I used these to get in here."

He looked behind him at the sliders, which were still slightly open. His movements allowed her to glimpse a flash of thigh. It was as toned as the rest of him, an observation that both pleased and alarmed her. Why should she care what shape he was in?

His eyes narrowed. "You know, if you'd come in the front door you'd probably have seen my truck outside and realized someone was home."

"That might be true, but again, it doesn't explain why you're in my cottage." She put her hands on her hips.

His mouth twitched like he was trying not to smile. "I *live* here."

"Oh. You're...renting this one?"

"No, it's included in my pay."

She put a hand to her forehead, trying to understand. "Then your employer is renting it?"

"Sure, if you want to call it that. Sadly, she's recently deceased so if you want confirmation, you're going to have to call her attorney. Speaking of, how did you get keys to this place? I'd ask if you're a Realtor, but I don't think most Realtors go around barefoot."

"Hold on," she said. "You said attorney. Do you mean Roger Gillum?" The pieces were starting to fall into place. Sort of.

"Yes, that's him."

"Which probably also means Norma Merriweather was your employer." Georgia was almost afraid to ask what her aunt had hired this man to do. Especially after learning how she'd befriended a town councilman to get her third-story exemption.

"She was. How do you know her?"

"She was my great aunt. And that's why this is now my cottage. And I have the keys." Georgia gave him another appraising look. "You still haven't told me who you are."

"Travis Taylor. And I was your aunt's handyman."

Georgia exhaled. "Oh. Handyman. Good." Then she frowned. "Um, based on the outside of the inn, your skills as a handyman seem questionable at best."

He crossed his arms over his chest and gave her a look. "I think we need to start from the beginning."

Maggie Miller

Chapter Eight

Travis knew he should go put some clothes on. It wasn't his way to be half-naked in the presence of a woman he didn't know. Or even those he did, unless there was something intimate going on between them. But he was wickedly delighted by this woman's inability to stop checking him out.

Wasn't every day a man his age got looked at like that by a woman who looked like her. But then, he didn't usually pay attention to the reactions of those around him.

This woman, however, was hard *not* to pay attention to. She was exceptionally pretty and had great legs. She also had an air about her that said she didn't suffer fools lightly. Norma had been that way too. Apparently, the apple didn't fall far from the tree. Which reminded him, he had no idea what this woman's name was.

"So you're Norma's grandniece?" The way he figured, she might be Georgia. That was the only relative Norma had ever spoken about with any affection so he couldn't imagine Norma leaving her estate to anyone else.

"I am. Georgia Carpenter."

"Nice to meet you, Georgia." His manners got the best of him. He hooked his thumb over his shoulder toward the bedroom. "You mind if I go put some clothes on?"

She shook her head. "I think that's a great idea. I'll wait right here."

"There's coffee if you want it. Help yourself."

"Thanks, I'm good."

He hustled to the bedroom, pulled on jeans and t-shirt, then went straight to the kitchen. She'd been true to her words and hadn't moved. He refilled his mug with coffee. He held it up. "You sure you don't want some?"

"No, I've had plenty this morning. Thanks."

"All right. How about we sit down in the living room and finish our talk?"

"Okay." She went straight to the chair.

He settled on the couch. "About my work as a handyman. When your aunt closed the inn because of her health, she stopped me from doing a lot of what needed to be done. Oh, she'd let me do small things, like fix a dripping faucet or change a lightbulb, but as things progressed, she didn't want the bother, as she put it. I think the noise aggravated her and she slept more during the day than she did most nights. So I understood."

"I see." But Georgia had a pained look on her face.

"Are you okay?"

She nodded. "I just wish I'd gotten over here to visit her before she passed." With a sigh, she lifted her chin. "The house looks like it hasn't been painted in years."

He nodded. "That's about right. Lot of other things haven't been done in years, either. But it wasn't my decision to make. Or my place to go against her wishes. She loved that house, loved running the inn, but at the end, her heart wasn't in it. And I loved her too much to argue."

"You loved her?"

He nodded. "Over the years, she became very dear to me."

Georgia seemed glad to hear that. "It's good to know that Norma wasn't completely alone in the end."

"She wasn't. Not as much as I could help it." Travis went on. "She let me keep up the two cottages but wouldn't allow me to do anything to the house. All she wanted was to join her beloved Cecil."

"Did you ever meet him?"

"No, he was well before my time."

"Of course." She crossed her legs under her. Reminding him of how shapely they were. "Based on your aunt's description of him and the tales she told, I wish I had met him. He's the reason she has all this. Had."

"I know. The attorney told me."

"It's all yours now, I take it?" He'd known this day would come. Already sadness filled him at the thought of leaving this wonderful spot.

"It is."

He'd have to find a place but affording something on the beach wasn't going to be possible. He'd have no choice but to move inland. He was going to miss this place so much. "I imagine you're going to sell it, huh?"

She shook her head. "No. I was hoping to get the inn up and running again. Aunt Norma left me the properties and some money. Enough, I hope, to do whatever needs to be done. Although I don't have a clue what that might be yet."

That was great news. Better than he'd expected, that was for sure. Well. Maybe it was. Maybe it wasn't. "I should tell you that your aunt left me some of Cecil's sports memorabilia. Just feels like something you should know."

"Thank you. I'm glad she left that to you."

"Also, I'd be happy to go over to the inn with you and do a walkthrough. We can figure it out together. Assuming you want to keep me on as the handyman."

"You said this cottage was included in your employment?"

"It is. Or was."

"That must make you more affordable."

He laughed. Just like Norma, getting to the bottom line right away. "You could look at it that way."

"And you must be good at what you do, or Aunt Norma wouldn't have kept you around."

He nodded. "She didn't have much tolerance for able slackers or willful idiots. Her words."

"That sounds like her." Georgia smiled, making her even prettier. "And no, she did not."

"So what do you say? You want to take a look around over there? See what needs to be done?"

"That would be great, but not yet. I promised my daughter I'd wait until she got back from her first day at Ludlows and then we'd look around together. Maybe tomorrow you and I can go through it?"

A daughter. So she was married. Maybe? There was no ring on her finger. Divorced then? Not that it was any of his business. Still he couldn't help but wonder. "It's a date."

She blushed. "Um, okay."

"Will your husband be joining us?"

"*No.*"

The sharp response made him quickly change the subject. "I'd love to get back in that house. I know there's a lot that needs doing."

"I'm sure there is." She glanced around. "You've kept this place up very well. And the other cottage."

He shrugged. "I didn't have much else to do. In the end, I sort of became her caretaker. At least until she went into the nursing home. But getting her groceries and picking up her prescriptions was better than doing nothing."

Georgia swallowed, her eyes suddenly luminous with unshed tears. "I should have been here. But I didn't know."

"Don't feel bad. She didn't want anyone to know. I can't tell you how many times I tried to get her to let me call someone. She wasn't having it. Didn't want family around her sobbing and crying and pretending to be sad just for a slice of her pie, as she'd say."

Georgia sniffed, but her smile returned. "That really sounds like her."

He sat back, stretching his arms across the couch cushions. "You were one of the only ones she talked about with any kindness or affection, so it's no wonder she left it all to you."

"She talked about me?"

"She did. Said you were one of the good ones."

Head down, she looked at her hands. "I don't know about that. But I did love her dearly. Coming to visit her when I was a kid was one of my favorite things to do. This place always seemed sort of magical to me, you know? I'm sure that sounds silly."

"Not at all. The beach definitely has its own magic. The sea and the salt and the sand are all ingredients in a potion that can cure whatever ails you. I think they are, anyway."

She picked her head up, interest lighting her blue eyes. "Did it cure you?"

That was a question he wasn't prepared to answer, but he wasn't going to lie to her either. "I'm getting there. Say, have you seen a big orange cat around?"

"Clyde?" She grinned. "He's been hanging out on our back deck."

"Okay, good. I figured he hadn't gone too far, but he's been a little scarcer than usual. Didn't see him all night. Thankfully, he showed up for breakfast this morning but took off again right after."

"I let him in during the storm last night. He was soaked. He was my aunt's cat?"

"He was. She loved him like you wouldn't believe. I'm a little surprised she didn't leave everything to him." He grinned. "I guess she liked you just a little bit more."

"I guess so." She laughed, and her cheeks went slightly pink again. "Sorry about walking in on you like I did. I really didn't know there was anyone home."

"I know. It's okay." As far as he was concerned, it was the most exciting thing that had happened to him in a long time. "I can see your aunt in you. A little around the eyes. And you have her laugh."

"I'll take that as a compliment. She was a remarkable woman. I owe her a lot."

As much as he wanted to dig into that comment, he left it alone. He didn't know her well enough to ask such personal questions and he figured when and if she wanted to talk, she would. So he just nodded. "That makes two of us."

Maggie Miller

Chapter Nine

Mia came home to find her mom sitting on the back deck in one of the Adirondack chairs. She had a worn paperback in her lap, but she was staring dreamily out at the water. Clyde was in the chair next to her, licking his paw and using it to clean his ear. "Hey there, I'm home."

Georgia looked up. "Hi, honey. How was it?"

"Great." Mia scooped Clyde into her arms so she could sit in the chair, but she held on to him and repositioned him on her lap. He stayed so he didn't seem too bothered by the adjustment. Or maybe the cheek scratches helped. "Learning the register was hard at first, because it's all computerized. But then something clicked and it just kind of made sense. They're going to put me on mornings, which I'm already not looking forward to, but it'll be fine once I get my sleep pattern changed around. Working nights has ruined me a little."

"You were up early this morning."

She made a face. "That's because Brendan called and woke me up."

"You didn't tell me that."

"I didn't talk to him so there was nothing to tell. I'm sure he just wants his ring back."

"I'm sure he wants *you* back."

"Well, that ain't happening." Mia instantly thought of Lucas. What that meant, she wasn't sure, but he was definitely better for her mood than Brendan. "I'll have to find the post office and ship that stupid thing back so this can be over. It's not like I'm ever going to wear it again."

"Probably not a bad idea. Make sure you get it insured or registered or whatever so he can't say it got lost."

"I will. But really, he's lucky I don't throw it into the ocean."

Georgia snorted. "Yes, he is." She glanced over. "You going to be all right working mornings?"

"Yep, totally. See the way I figure it, the best part about working mornings is I'll have the rest of my day free. Which means I'll be able to work a second job. At least until you need me at the inn."

"I hate to think about you working so much."

"Mom, right now they're only giving me three shifts a week. I can definitely take on a second job somewhere. Three shifts are barely going to pay for my gas and insurance."

"You could always ride a bike."

"That's actually not a bad idea, except I'd have to buy one first." Mia inspected her mother a little closer. Georgia looked happier than she had when she'd been telling Mia about inheriting the inn. Well, maybe not happier but there was a new layer of happiness. Something that didn't have to do with the beach or the inn. Mia narrowed her eyes. "You didn't go in the house without me, did you?"

"No! I promise." Georgia smiled. "What makes you think that?"

"You look...I don't know, like you're hiding a good secret."

Georgia shrugged. "Just had a nice day is all."

"Oh?" That seemed like a pretty vague answer, but Mia didn't really know how nice her mother's day could be just from looking around the other cottage. Unless that wasn't what she'd done. "Did you go to the second cottage?"

"I did. It's in...great shape."

"That's good." Mia narrowed her eyes. "Why are you smiling like that?"

"No reason. Oh, I, uh, met Aunt Norma's handyman."

Mia hesitated, picturing some gruff old dude in a worn ballcap and three days of stubble. "And?"

Georgia stared out at the sea, her smile a little coy and her eyes lit with the most curious glow. "He's nice."

Mia mentally erased the picture of the gruff old dude. "Yeah, back up. Nice people don't make you glow."

"I'm not glowing."

"Mom. For real. What's up?"

"He's an attractive man. That's all."

Mia laughed. "Mom, are you crushing on Mr. Toolbelt?"

"One, he was not wearing a toolbelt." For some reason, that statement seemed to make her mother blush. "And two, no. I'm not crushing on anyone. I'm not even officially divorced from your father yet. The last thing I want is a boyfriend. I mean it. I need some time to find myself again and just be me. As new-agey as that sounds."

Mia nodded. "I think that's a great plan. Doesn't hurt that he's easy to look at, though, right?"

"Doesn't matter what he looks like. What matters is he's eager to help with fixing up the inn."

"Speaking of, are you ready to go over and have a look around?"

Georgia nodded. "Definitely. Do you want to change first?"

Mia glanced down at her outfit. "Yeah, I probably should. I don't want to get my new shirt dirty. No telling what it's like over there and I only have this one. Gimme a sec."

"No problem. I want to find a notebook and a pen so I can start a list of what needs to be done."

Mia put Clyde down on the deck as she stood.

He took two steps, then laid down.

She laughed. "That is one chill cat."

"Oh, that reminds me." Georgia closed the book and got up. "Travis said Clyde was absolutely Aunt Norma's cat and that she loved him dearly. He said he was surprised she didn't leave everything to him."

"Travis?"

"Mr. Toolbelt."

Mia smirked. "Just how long did you hang out with him?"

"Just a little. Settle down. He lives in the other cottage, by the way. It's part of his employment package."

"And he knows you're his new employer?"

"He does. Now go get changed or you can stay home with Clyde."

"Nice try," Mia said as she headed into her bedroom. "But you are not leaving me behind and we are not done talking about Travis."

"Whatever," her mother playfully answered back.

Mia grinned. It was nice to see her mother in such a good mood. For too long, she had been miserable because of the divorce. And rightly so. It had been messy and contentious and all around ugly. Still was. And all her father's fault, as far as Mia was concerned. He was the one who'd cheated. He was the one who had broken the marriage vows. He was the one who'd destroyed their family.

Because of that, Mia hadn't really spoken to her father since his affair had come to light.

She was still mad at him. Probably would be for quite a while. How did you get over the fact that your father's extramarital needs had ruined your life? What he'd done had been selfish. Just like Brendan.

Mia shook her head as she took off her Ludlows polo shirt, hung it up, then pulled on the Wonder Woman T-shirt she'd worn earlier. Lucas was cute, but she suddenly realized she needed to do the same thing her mother was doing. Take some time for herself. Be single for a while.

If Lucas was still around and available when she was ready to get back into dating, so be it. If he wasn't, well, as the saying went, there were other fish out there.

And she now lived in a cottage right next to the sea.

Maggie Miller

Chapter Ten

Armed with only one set of keys, Georgia and Mia took the sidewalk over to the house that sat abandoned between them and the other cottage. There was a pretty little white fence out front.

Or at least the fence *had* been white. Like the trim on the house, it had peeled and weathered to a dingy shade of gray. Some kind of vine-like weed had taken over about half of it as well and one of the pickets was cracked.

But then, the whole place was in desperate shape, something that was now very obvious up close. Even the sign was missing from the metal post that had obviously once held it.

The grass in the yard was mostly filled with weeds and was knee high, the shrubs had lost their shape, the crepe myrtles at the front of the property were in desperate need of a trim, and the flower boxes were just bare dirt. The wind chime hanging off the porch only had two pipes left on it. The porch railing was missing a baluster, and also needed to be repainted.

The house was built on short piers or pilings, setting it off the ground about two feet. The lattice that covered that space was just as faded as the rest of the place, but it also had some holes in it. And some sections were missing. It might all have to be replaced.

Alongside of the house, the parking lot looked more like it was becoming part of the yard, the oyster shells that paved it nearly invisible under the tall grass and thick weeds that had cropped up. If there had ever been lines or parking spot indicators, they were long gone.

There was so much work to do.

Even so, it was easy to see what a gorgeous, welcoming place this had once been. Georgia could effortlessly imagine welcoming guests into this house. She couldn't wait to see what it looked like inside, and if she could still picture how pretty the interior had been too, once upon a time.

Mia put her hand on the fence gate. "This yard is going to be a major project."

"It's all going to be a major project. But we'll get it done." Georgia peered up at the house. "We'll get it all done. You'll see."

Mia's smirk came back. "With Travis's help, you mean."

Georgia just shook her head. "Get a hold of yourself, child." She laughed as she pushed the gate open. The hinges creaked as they resisted the movement. They'd need to be oiled, at least. Maybe replaced. "Come on, let's go inside."

They went down the paver-stone path, which was also overgrown, and up to the porch. The steps seemed sturdy, but a few of the railings looked wobbly. While she was inspecting it, she noticed something tucked behind the unkempt shrubs.

"Hey, look." She pointed. "I think that's the sign for the inn."

Mia went down to inspect, wading through the tall grass. Georgia hoped there weren't any snakes in there. Mia grabbed the corner of the thing and dragged it out to lay it flat on the yard. "Yep, that's exactly what it is."

Maybe because the sign had been protected behind the shrubs, but it didn't seem to have weathered as much as the house. In clear lettering done in pale blue and ocean green against a white background, it read *The Sea Glass Inn.* Then in smaller letters, *Proprietor, Norma Merriweather.*

Georgia smiled. "I can't wait until we can hang that up again. With our names on it."

Mia wiped her hands on her shorts. "Me, too."

"Although maybe we can find a way to keep Aunt Norma's name as a part of it."

"That would be nice," Mia said.

Georgia gazed up at the inn. "Let's see just how much work this place is going to take."

They went up the porch steps and she got the keys out. She found the right one on the second try as Mia stood by watching. Georgia opened the door.

"Oh," Mia said. "It's beautiful."

Georgia nodded as they stepped inside and took it all in. "Now this is more like Aunt Norma. Needs a good airing out."

"For sure."

But beautiful was the right word despite the fact that drop cloths covered most of the furniture. There were still enough things visible to get a sense of what the house had once looked like. And to get a feel for Aunt Norma's unique style. Even if a slight musty odor permeated the air.

First and foremost was the big blown glass and crystal chandelier that hung in the foyer. It was coated with grime and would take a careful cleaning to sparkle again, but it was easy to see what a showstopper it could be. In part because it was designed to look like a blue octopus, each tentacle curling out from the body and holding a multitude of clear crystal drops.

Looking past the dust and disuse, the house had a charming, Southern seaside vibe. Old Florida with a touch of shabby chic and great taste in antiques thrown in.

Warm, wide plank wood floors were covered with beautiful, intricately woven rugs. One had shells in the pattern. Another that Georgia could see had fish. Those would need to be vacuumed, maybe even shampooed, and the wood polished, but that was all part of the process of bringing the house back to life.

She started jotting things down on the notebook she'd brought. A set of wide steps went up to the second floor from the foyer. The stairs were the same color as the wood planks, but the railings and balusters were painted white.

At the second floor, another set of steps led from the landing to the third floor.

On their level, a hall led past the stairs into the rear of the house, but on either side of the foyer were openings that showed off a grand living room on one side and a spacious dining room on the other. The living room was so large it had two different seating areas. The dining room even with its table and chairs covered over, looked like it could effortlessly seat twelve.

"Which way do you want to go first?" Georgia asked.

Mia shook her head. "I don't know. I want to look at all of it. Right now."

Georgia laughed. "I feel the same way." She pointed to the living room. "Let's go that way. I think all of these rooms probably feed into the next so we can probably make a loop."

Mia nodded. "Sounds good to me. I'm not sure one trip around is going to be enough."

"Don't forget, there are two more floors."

"And I can't wait to see them. Do you know which one Aunt Norma lived on? Where her room was?"

"Not a clue. I'm sure we'll figure it out when we come to it."

They started through the living room, looking under the drop cloths, trying light switches, peeking in drawers and cabinets. The house felt like a treasure box waiting to be discovered. There was so much to see.

From the long living room, they came back out into the hall which led into a bright, sunny room filled with tables.

"The breakfast room?" Mia said.

"Maybe." Georgia looked out the wall of glass doors to the beach beyond. "Great view to take in first thing in the morning."

"I'll say." Mia pointed to a doorway at the side of the room with a swinging half-door covering it. "Kitchen?"

"I bet," Georgia said.

They went through. It was.

The kitchen was big and had good bones. It also had a large industrial style stainless steel stove with double ovens, and an equally large double-door refrigerator. Big stainless-steel sink, too. Other than those things, it felt dated. Georgia thought that might be easy to fix. Some new cabinet hardware, maybe. New flooring. Maybe even some upgraded light fixtures. But then again, did any of that matter as long as the appliances were in good, working order? The guests weren't really going to see the kitchen, were they?

But it brought to mind another question. Who was going to do the cooking? Guests would at least expect breakfast, wouldn't they? The room filled with tables seemed to suggest that.

Mia nudged her mom. "You look deep in thought all of a sudden."

Georgia continued to study the kitchen. "I was thinking about the fact that we're going to need a cook. I think. I don't know what Aunt Norma did, but I'm guessing people are going to expect breakfast based on that room next door. Right? Or not?"

"Probably. But don't you think we could handle that? Especially if we kept it simple?"

"Maybe in the beginning, but not if things get rolling and we have a full house. That's a lot of people to feed." A tiny bit of anxiety took hold in Georgia's belly. "And then there are all the rooms to clean, laundry to do, guests to deal with—"

"Mom, we can do it. People run inns and B&Bs all over the country. There are services you can get for laundry. And staff you can hire for the rest of it. I know in the beginning, it's going to be mostly just us, but we'll start slow. We'll put my degree to the test. And we'll do as much as we can do until we can afford to hire more help."

Georgia nodded. "You're right. Thank you." She grabbed Mia's hand. "See? I told you I was going to need you."

Mia's gaze was alight with eagerness. "I can't wait."

"I'm glad to hear that." Georgia made a note to talk to Travis about putting the kitchen renovation on hold. Unless it could be done cheaply.

Guestrooms and common rooms would be more important immediately and depending on what things cost, they were going to have to prioritize.

A door off of the kitchen took them into a good-sized bedroom with its own bathroom and access to what seemed to be a small, private side porch. The bedroom had an antique brass bed, but the rest of the furniture was a mix of things painted white and some more antiques. A bright blue rocking chair had pride of place in the corner.

"This looks like it was Aunt Norma's room," Mia said.

Georgia nodded. "Definitely. It smells like the perfume she always used to wear." There were a few photos around, one of Georgia as a baby that made her suck in a breath when she realized that's what it was. How sweet. There was another of a slightly smaller Clyde sitting by a Christmas tree. She held that picture up. "Clearly Aunt Norma loved that cat."

Mia smiled. "Look how cute he is. Do you think he misses her?"

"Probably." Georgia sighed. "I do."

"Is it hard for you to be here?"

"A little. Makes me feel like I missed out on so much of her life that I should have been a part of, if that makes sense. She left me all of this and I don't feel deserving of such an amazing gift."

"You are, or she wouldn't have left it to you."

"It's kind of you to say that." But Georgia knew the only way to make this right was to bring the inn back to life and honor Aunt Norma's legacy by making it thrive again.

Mia opened the closet. It wasn't full, but what was there was mostly bright and colorful. Mia closed the door, then looked around. "You know, this room isn't in bad shape. It really just needs to be cleaned up and emptied out. You could totally move in here. And if there's another room that would work for me, then we could both live here while we rehab the place." She turned, smiling. "Which means you could rent our cottage out and get some money coming in right away."

"That's a great idea," Georgia said. "But first we have to make sure this place is okay for occupancy. I don't want to find out there's a hole in the roof or the electrical isn't sound and then we're homeless because there's already someone in the cottage."

Mia made a sassy face at her. "I'm sure you could always stay with Travis."

Georgia snorted, despite not wanting to laugh. "You're not going to let that go, are you?"

Mia shook her head. "Nope. Not just yet." She grinned. "Let's go check out the rest of this place."

On their way, they took a longer look at the breakfast room. It was a bright space with white walls, pale blue gingham valances over its many windows and two sets of

French doors that led out to the magnificent deck Georgia had seen from the beach. There were a few tables for two, several more that could seat four, and one large communal table in the center. Simple crystal chandeliers gave the room a slightly French country feeling. There wasn't anything about it Georgia wanted to change.

The wall that divided the room from the kitchen held a long, pale blue server. Georgia pointed to it. "That's probably where the breakfast buffet was set up."

"I bet you're right." Mia turned slowly, taking it all in. She stopped and looked at something on the interior wall. "What's that door lead to?"

Georgia shook her head. "Open it."

And as it turned out, there was a small foyer space that had three more doors.

One led to a twin of Aunt Norma's room, one led to an enormous walk-in pantry and the other to a laundry room. The second bedroom was a tiny bit smaller and the bathroom only had a shower instead of the tub *and* shower that Norma's had, and there was no side porch, but Mia declared it perfect for her.

From there, a second, smaller hall led to a room made up as a library. Beside that was a powder room, and then back around to the big dining room. Both the dining room and long living room had doors that opened onto the wrap-around front porch.

Georgia could just see lots of rocking chairs out there. What a great place to hang out that would be on balmy summer evenings.

The second floor had five bedrooms, all with their own bathrooms. Each room had a name instead of a number and they were all decorated accordingly. Several of them needed some updating.

Then they took the last flight of steps up to the third floor, the one Aunt Norma had beguiled a town councilman into letting her have.

Georgia was so glad Norma had made that happen, however she'd done it. The view from the single, expansive suite was breathtaking. The space had one good sized bedroom, a very nice bathroom and a sitting room.

"Oh, this is a honeymoon suite if I ever saw one," Mia said.

"You think?"

She nodded. "This is a premium space. Trust me. Before Brendan screwed up, I'd been looking at places for the honeymoon. Throw in a bottle of champagne, some chocolate covered strawberries and rose petals on the bed, and you could get top dollar for a suite like this."

"Funny you should say that, because I was thinking earlier about adding a gazebo in the back because it might entice small wedding parties. Weddings could be very good for business. Especially if we can get a florist and bakery to work out a package with us."

"See? Now you're thinking like a businesswoman. And there is a florist in town, I saw it across the street from Ludlows." Suddenly Mia frowned. "How do you know there's space in the back for a gazebo? I thought you didn't come over here without me?"

"I didn't. That was just an observation on my way up the beach to Travis's."

"Oh. Well, it's a really good idea."

"If the budget allows."

Mia put her hands on her hips. "We should make sure it allows. There is money in weddings."

"I have no doubt." Georgia sighed as she looked around. "But there is a lot of cleaning and updating to do. A lot."

"And I'm pretty sure I heard at least one dripping faucet. Or a running toilet. Or both."

"The good news is we know the water works." Georgia laughed, then she shook her head. "This feels a little overwhelming."

"It does. But you know what? There's no real time frame."

"Except there kind of is," Georgia corrected her. "If we don't get this place ready by the start of the tourist season, we'll lose a lot of revenue."

"Hmm." Mia pursed her mouth. "I hadn't thought of that. But that's more than six months away."

Georgia shook her head. "We can't wait that long. We need to get open sooner. While people still want to escape winter up north."

"Then I guess it's time to get Travis over here so he can tell us the truth."

Georgia smiled. "You really want to meet him, don't you?"

Mia lifted one shoulder, her smile extra sweet. "That too."

Maggie Miller

Chapter Eleven

Travis opened the door to find Georgia and another young woman standing there. Her daughter, he guessed. He smiled at Georgia. "Well, look at you using the front door."

Georgia smirked at him. "Travis, this is my daughter, Mia. Mia, this is Travis Taylor. Aunt Norma's handyman."

He stuck his hand out to shake Mia's. "Your handyman, now."

Mia's grin seemed bigger than necessary, but maybe she was nervous. Although her smile looked more like she knew a joke he didn't.

Had Georgia told her daughter about his towel-only appearance? He'd find that hard to believe.

She glanced at her mom, still smiling, before taking his hand. "Nice to meet you, Travis."

"You, too, Mia." His gaze returned to Georgia. Her daughter was pretty, but he preferred the tree that apple had fallen from. "I take it this isn't a social call?"

Georgia held up a notebook. "We've had a look around the inn and I've made a list of what I think needs doing, but we're ready for your professional assessment."

"All right. Let's have a look. I just need to get some shoes on. Tomorrow I can do a thorough inspection of the outside and the roof."

"Sounds good." Georgia leaned on the door jamb while he stuck his feet in some boat shoes.

Together, the three of them walked to the inn. As they went up the path to the porch, he nodded at the sign, still laying in the yard. "I can get that hung back up when you're ready."

Georgia glanced at it. "We should probably wait until we're closer to opening, don't you think?"

"Whatever you want. But how about we put it on the porch for now? It'll kill the grass if it lays there too long."

Georgia nodded. "Sure. About that grass…"

He hefted the sign onto his shoulder and carried it up, leaning it against the wall of the house. "I know, trust me. Last time I tried to mow it your aunt yelled at me for making too much noise. But now that you're in charge, I'll get it taken care of."

"Thanks," Georgia said as she and Mia came up the steps. "That will help a lot. But actually, I think I could tackle the landscaping. It's just weeding and trimming. Lots of it. But nothing all that complicated. After all, you're probably going to have bigger things to tend to that I couldn't begin to handle."

"True. Do you have the key?" Travis asked.

"We left the door unlocked," Mia said.

"All right." He opened it but waited for them to go ahead of him. He surveyed the space before him, remembering what it used to look like. "Things sure have gotten dusty."

"Did you put all these drop cloths over everything?" Georgia asked.

"I did." It felt good to be in the old place, Travis thought. But it was a little sad to see it closed up and in need of so much help. "It was the last official thing I did for your aunt as her handyman."

After that, all he'd been able to do was run small errands for her. She'd allowed nothing else. No matter how hard he'd tried.

"I'm glad she had the forethought to have you do it," Georgia said. "Probably saved a lot of the furniture from needing to be cleaned. How long has it been since you've been in here?"

"I'd say a year. Maybe longer. But the inn was shut down well before that."

"How long?" Mia asked.

He thought a moment. "The last guest probably checked out close to three years ago. But business had been slipping for several years already. As Norma declined, she didn't want to do much. Can't say as I blamed her, what with her health failing and all. And then she went into the nursing home and that was that."

Georgia nodded in clear understanding, eyes a little damp. "Well, I want to do her proud. What do you think needs doing?"

"What doesn't need doing?"

Georgia laughed softly. "Well...where do we start?"

"Place needs airing out for one thing."

Georgia and Mia both nodded. Georgia asked, "How do we know that musty smell isn't mold?"

"Getting some fresh air in here will help us determine that, but I'll check for it too in all the usual places," he said. "But let's keep a good thought that's not the problem."

"Right," Georgia said. "What else?"

"The place will need a deep cleaning. All surfaces. From ceiling fans to baseboards and everything in between. Floors polished. Rugs vacuumed at a minimum, but they may need to be beaten and shampooed too. There might be a couple that aren't salvageable. Same goes for the window treatments. Some might need to be replaced if moths have gotten after them or if they've faded too much to be presentable. Everything needs to be inspected upstairs as well too."

Georgia alternated between scribbling things onto her list and checking other items off.

He gave her a second to catch up, then kept going. "That's just cosmetics, though. The HVAC will need to be checked. It's still functioning as far as I know."

"Seems all right in here to me," Mia said. "I mean, it's a little stuffy, but not hot."

He nodded. "No, but then it's cooler this time of year already. A few more months and you're going to want the heat to work."

"True," she said.

"Anyway, my guess is the HVAC will at least need recharging. Hopefully, that's it. If it needs replacing, then you're in for a mighty steep bill."

Georgia grimaced. "I guess it's a good thing Norma left me some money."

"It is," he said. "But I'd hate to see it all used up for something like that. Same goes for the roof. It should have six or seven more years left on it, but until I look at it...who knows. You didn't see any water damage while you were inspecting the place, did you?"

Georgia looked at Mia, who shrugged. "We weren't really looking for that, sorry."

"It's all right. I'll figure it out."

Mia wrinkled her nose. "Could that be what we're smelling? That mustiness? Could it be from water that's seeped in?"

He shook his head. "I don't think so. If there was mold, the smell would be a lot stronger. My professional guess is that it's just regular damp from the house being shut up. A couple days with the windows open and most of that should be gone."

"That's a relief," Georgia said. "Let's go have a look at the kitchen next."

They walked through and memories came rushing into Travis's mind. Thoughts of happier times and a lot of laughter. Norma had been a great boss. She was quite a character, but he'd loved being part of her team. They'd spent many a night sitting on her private deck, sharing a drink while he listened to one of her entertaining stories.

He'd always told her she should write a book, but she'd brushed off the suggestion every time.

Maybe he could pass some of those stories on. Especially now that he knew Georgia and her daughter weren't going to sell the place. That thrilled him. Seemed to him that a house this extraordinary should remain in the care of family. People who understood how special it was and wanted to look after it. People who could appreciate the woman who'd started it.

And the legacy she'd left behind.

They entered the kitchen and he smiled at the familiar space. "I tried to get her to update this room for years, but she said it was better to use the money on the rooms the guests spent their time in."

Georgia laughed. "I was kind of thinking the same thing. But I also thought that as long as all the appliances were in good shape, maybe a little freshening up wouldn't be such a big deal. Like new cabinet hardware."

He nodded. "And I'd get rid of those awful fluorescents overhead, too. That light is terrible. Wouldn't be that big of a project to lay in a simple tile floor, either. The room is basically a rectangle. And this linoleum has seen better days."

Georgia nodded. "You and I are definitely on the same page with this room. But I don't think it's going on the top of the list. Anything that needs to be done in a guest room or a common room has to come first."

"I understand," he said. She was a lot like her aunt. He considered that a good thing. "You want to get open as soon as possible."

"It's not even that I want to so much as we have to. The money she left me isn't going to last forever. We need to get some coming in."

"Oh, as the sole employee, I couldn't agree with you more." He stuck his thumbs through the belt loops on his jeans. "I don't want to be downsized."

They all laughed.

Mia pointed at the fridge. "How are the appliances? They don't look brand new, but they look like they're in good shape. Certainly better than this floor. We weren't brave enough to open the fridge, just in case it was a horror show inside."

Travis shook his head. "I don't know about that, but horror show might be a good guess. I don't think it's been cleaned out since Norma last lived here. I certainly didn't do it. She would have given me a talking to if I'd even attempted it. Hopefully, the appliances should be good though. They're all industrial grade, bought at an auction when a local restaurant closed down. Again, I can check them all out tomorrow."

Mia continued. "Speaking of employees, what did Aunt Norma do for a cook and laundry service? And housekeeping?"

"She had a company that took care of the linens and she had a cook, but Berta retired when Norma closed the inn. For housekeeping, she had a couple of women from town that took care of that. All of that information, for what it's still worth, should be in her office."

Georgia and Mia looked at each other for a second, then Georgia shrugged. "We didn't find an office."

"That doesn't surprise me. She liked it that way mostly so guests couldn't bother her when she was doing bills, she used to say. She also frowned at me when I called it her lair." He grinned. "Follow me."

He led them out of the kitchen and half-way down the hall to where the stairs were at about head-height in front of them. The area underneath the stairs was walled off with decorative panels, but at the tallest point, facing them, was one very special panel.

He pushed on it and it popped open, revealing it as a secret door.

Mia gasped. "That is *so* cool. It's like Harry Potter."

"It's like Norma Merriweather," Georgia said.

"That it is." With a smile, Travis opened it all the way, then reached in and turned on the light. There was just enough space under the stairs for a built-in desk with two drawers on one side and a chair. Above the desk where the ceiling sloped, was a single shelf lined with ledger books. The desk was still piled with papers and odds and ends. On the sidewall was a corkboard with all sorts of things stuck on it. "There you go, your aunt's office."

"That is so clever," Georgia said. "I can just picture her squirreled away in there, doing her bookkeeping and going over her paperwork."

Travis could see Norma there too. "She kept great records. One of those ledgers has a daily documentation of the weather, the number of guests at the inn that day, and sometimes a few other notes about what was going on."

"You know," Mia said. "You can look up the weather for any day on the internet."

He snorted. "I realize that, but your aunt was not a fan of computers. You won't find one in this house."

"Oh!" Mia turned toward Georgia. "Mom. Put this on your list. We need to make sure we have Wi-Fi for the guests."

Travis wondered what Norma would think of that, but he supposed it was inevitable if the inn was going to stay current. "You're on your own for that one."

"About breakfast," Georgia started after she'd added Mia's note. "Do we have to offer that to guests?"

"No," Travis said. "But in a place like this, they'll expect something. Doesn't have to be fancy, though. Some cold cereal, pastries, fruit. Most people will be happy enough with that and if they aren't, they can go into town to the Fork & Spoon. I think the diner would be glad for the business, too. But they'll be glad for any business you bring in and people will definitely go there for lunch and dinner."

"Good to know," Georgia said. "We could probably get open sooner if we didn't need to hire a cook right away. What did Norma do?"

"Berta cooked a full breakfast every morning. Eggs, waffles or pancakes, fried potatoes, grits some days, bacon and sausage, ham if there was left over from a holiday. Toast, of course. Pastries or muffins sometimes. Homemade jam. And then cold stuff like cereal and fruit. On weekends, she might add a crockpot of steel-cut oats or a tray of cinnamon buns."

"Quite a spread," Georgia said.

"I'll say." Mia's brows rose as she put a hand on her stomach. "Just hearing about it has made me hungry."

Maggie Miller

Gulf Coast Cottage

Chapter Twelve

Georgia laughed, but her stomach had rumbled too. Hard not to after all that mention of food. "Same here. But we'll be done in a bit and we can go eat."

Mia rubbed her hands together. "We're having a big celebratory dinner tonight, Travis. You want to come over? We're having steak."

Travis's eyebrows shot up in surprise. "That's really kind of you, but I wouldn't want to intrude."

Georgia looked at her daughter. Was Mia trying to encourage something? Georgia wasn't sure, but it was nice of her to have asked Travis. "You should come, Travis. We'd love to have you. So long as you don't mind talking about Aunt Norma or the house."

"I wouldn't mind that at all." He seemed to be thinking about it. "But only if I can bring something. How about salad and dessert?"

"That's two things," Mia said.

He nodded. "And they're both coming from Ludlows so don't get too excited."

Georgia laughed. "That would be great. That's kind of you."

He smiled at her. "Just trying to butter up the boss."

She smiled back. Truth be told, there wasn't much buttering to do. She liked Travis. He was a nice guy, and it didn't hurt that he was easy to look at. Plus, she liked that he was about the same age as her. If he'd been a younger guy, she might not have had so much faith in him until he proved himself.

Of course, it also helped that Aunt Norma had considered him a friend. It was plain to see why, too, based on the things Travis had said. He'd clearly been a friend to her. Georgia might have missed out on Aunt Norma's last days, but she knew the woman well enough to know that she wouldn't have allowed Travis to help her with things if she didn't trust him.

Certainly not with getting her prescriptions or taking care of Clyde.

"We should finish up the house," Georgia said. "Then maybe over dinner we can make our plan of attack."

Travis nodded. "Sounds good. Is there anything else you want to look at on this floor?"

"Not that I can think of," Georgia said.

"All right. Let's head upstairs."

The rest of the house tour was pretty simple. They'd go into each room, have a look around, Travis would check that the lights were all working and have Georgia note any bulbs that needed changing, then he'd inspect the ceiling for signs of water.

Thankfully, there weren't any so far.

He also flushed all the toilets and ran the taps in every bathroom. He came out of the one attached to the fifth bedroom. "The valve in that toilet is going to need changing."

Georgia wrote it down. "That makes three."

"Might be smart to just change them all so the rest don't start leaking too. That's what happens when a house sits, and toilets don't get flushed. Valves rot."

"Good to know," Mia said. "I feel like I'm learning all kinds of things."

Travis nodded. "You should learn some basic maintenance. Especially if you're going to help your mom run this place. It's just handy to know."

"Will you teach me?" she asked.

"I'd be happy to. Want to start with the valves? They're pretty easy to do. We could knock them out tomorrow."

"Sure. So long as you can wait until I get off of work."

"Not a problem. There is plenty to keep me busy."

"Cool. Thanks." Mia looked pleased.

Georgia was too. Travis's generosity was not unnoticed. Teaching Mia a new skill would definitely make replacing the valves go slower, but he didn't seem to care. Maybe he was just a generous guy. But then again, Aunt Norma had obviously liked him for a reason.

"All right," Georgia said. "Should we head upstairs and check out the last room?"

They both nodded at her.

As they went up the steps, Mia asked another question. "Did Aunt Norma ever use this suite for honeymooners? Seems like it would be perfect for that."

"She might have," Travis answered. "I didn't always know that much about the guests that stayed here unless there was a problem in their room. But you're right, the suite would be great for that. Might even charge a little extra for it, if you set it up right."

Mia gave Georgia a look. "See? I said the same thing."

"Uh oh," Travis said. He was looking up. "That could be a little water damage right there. See how the paint on the ceiling is a little discolored? Like tea's been spilled on it?"

Georgia's heart sank. "That's bad, isn't it?"

"It's not great, but considering how long this place has sat, it's better than what I expected to find. I'll get on that first thing."

"We're on the third floor," Mia said. "Isn't it kind of high up?"

He laughed. "Yes, but there's no other way to handle it but get on the roof to repair and reshingle that section. Don't worry, I've been on this roof quite a few times over the years without any issue."

Georgia wasn't so sure she liked the idea either. "How about if I come over and just keep an eye out?"

He looked at her. "You mean so that if I fall to my death, the body won't lay there too long?"

She laughed, despite the morbid thought. "That's not what I meant. Well, I guess it sort of was. I could at least hold the ladder."

"That would be nice. I'd gladly take the help." He went about his usual inspection, checking lights, testing the taps, flushing the toilet. He frowned. "Add another flapper valve to the list."

Mia walked over to the big windows that faced the gulf and stared out. "The view from up here is amazing. Look at it. It's almost like you can't tell where the sea stops and the sky begins."

Georgia jotted down the note about the valve, then joined her daughter. "It's something else, isn't it? Hard to stop looking at it. We're so lucky to live here."

"That is quite a view." Behind them, Travis's stomach growled. He laughed. "Sorry. Guess I'm more ready for dinner than I thought."

Georgia looked over her shoulder. "We're all done here, right?"

He nodded. "For a first pass, we covered a lot. That punch list will keep us busy for a long time."

"How long?"

"You mean before you can open?"

She nodded.

He thought a moment. "If we work really hard and nothing major needs to be replaced...maybe a month or two."

"Okay, then that's our goal. Reopen in two months. What do you think, Mia? Can you get everything done on your end by then? All the business stuff?"

"Sure. I think. I'll do my best. But that means December. Don't you think that's a tough month to get business?"

"I'm okay with starting slow." Georgia clipped her pen to her notebook. "Now let's call it a day and get to work on dinner."

Less than an hour later, Travis was at the door of their cottage, a cloth Ludlows bag in one hand and a bouquet of flowers in the other.

He held them out to Georgia. "Norma always said you should bring something when you get invited to a meal."

She smiled as she took the flowers. "You already brought dessert and a salad."

"Something that was for the hostess. Not for the meal. Like a bottle of wine that was for the hostess to enjoy later."

"Oh, did you bring wine, too?" Georgia teased.

"No, but I did bring a six pack of beer for myself, just in case you didn't have any." He pulled the six pack out of the Ludlows bag.

"Good thinking," she said. "We don't have any." She stepped out of the way. "Come on in. Mia's on the back deck, feeding Clyde some treats she brought home for him earlier."

"What can I do to help? Want me to start the grill?"

"Actually, that would be great. My husband always did all the grilling and I'm a little afraid I might singe my eyebrows off trying to start it."

"Can't have that," Travis said. "I'll get it going." He put the grocery bag on the table and headed for the deck.

Georgia unpacked the bag as Travis went outside. He'd picked up a chopped veggie salad with vinaigrette that looked like it had come from a cold foods case and a chocolate silk pie that had to be from the bakery. He'd even thought to get a small can of whipped cream. She nodded in approval. "Aunt Norma has taught you well."

She put them all in the fridge, then went to get the tray of steaks to carry them outside. She found Travis at the grill and Mia feeding the last of the treats to Clyde, who was pawing at her with such cuteness Georgia had to smile. What great company he must have been for Aunt Norma.

She put the tray down on the table under the little covered area, then joined Travis at the grill. "Do you know how to turn these overhead lights on? I couldn't find the switch. I'm guessing it's in the same spot at your place."

"Should be. Look behind the curtains on the left side of the living room. Should be on the right, but I didn't build these cottages. Actually, you live in Norma's original one so maybe it's on the correct side."

"Okay, let me check." She went inside and found the switch on the left where he'd said it would be. She flipped it and the bulbs came to life with a pleasing golden glow. She stepped out of the cottage smiling. "Thank you, that worked. Same place, left side."

"Mom, they're so pretty."

Georgia nodded. "They are, aren't they." She looked at Travis. "Does the inn have these?"

"No." Travis held his hand over the grill, testing the heat. "Always meant to put them up but never got around to it before your aunt got sick. We can add it to the list, though. You can change the colors too. If you can find the remote."

"That reminds me," Georgia said. "About my list. I need to go get my notebook and we can work on our plan. Be right back. Would you like a beer while I'm in there?"

"Sure, thanks. Grill needs a few more minutes to warm up."

She went inside, grabbed her notebook, her pen, and a beer for him. She handed him the bottle when she returned. Then she took a seat in one of the Adirondack chairs, pen poised over the paper. "What's first?"

"For you or for me? Because those are two different lists."

She thought about that. "Right. Let's start with you. Although I suppose you don't really need a list."

"I don't mind. I'm all in favor of staying organized. Plus it'll help you keep track of what I'm working on. You can put inspect and repair roof at the top. That has to happen immediately. We don't want any more water damage than what's already there."

"That's for sure." She jotted that down. "What about painting? That's going to be a big job."

"It is and it's more than I can handle. It's going to require tools and equipment I don't have. Scaffolding especially. But I have a buddy that can handle it."

"Shouldn't we get more than one bid?" She didn't want to step on Travis's toes, but she wanted to know what her options were. And make sure she got the best price.

"We can. There's a painter a few towns over who should be decent too."

"I'm not saying we won't go with your friend, but…"

He nodded. "I know. You want to be smart with your money. I want the same thing. I'm on the payroll, remember? Besides, it might help my friend to sharpen his pencil a little if he knows he's got competition."

"Right." She smiled. "Okay, what's next on the list?"

Chapter Thirteen

Mia watched her mom and Travis together, surprised by how much their playful interaction pleased her. It was nice to see her mom laugh and have fun. It was even nicer to see her with a new exciting goal. The inn was going to be a project for sure. But the end result would be life changing.

Mia wondered if her mother's relationship with Travis would be just as life changing. Not that she hoped her mom would rush off and get married or anything like that. But it would be nice for her to have a dependable man in her life.

And Travis definitely seemed dependable. After all, he'd stuck by Aunt Norma, hadn't he? That alone earned him points in Mia's mind.

What other man would have done that? Besides Clyde. Certainly not one who wasn't a relative. No, Travis was a good guy. The kind of guy her mom deserved. So what if he wasn't a doctor or a lawyer or some fancy businessman. Mia's own father had been a CEO of a tech firm and look what that had gotten them.

A man with a taste for excess and enough money to think he could do whatever he wanted.

In comparison, Travis seemed like a saint.

Her mom glanced over at her. "You want a glass of wine? I'm going to get one for myself."

"That would be great," Mia answered. "I got a rosé. Let's have that. It feels the most festive."

"Sounds good to me. Be right back." Her mom went inside.

Mia went back to thinking about men. Lucas in particular. He seemed kind of halo worthy, too. He'd been so sweet and patient with her at work. He'd personally taught her the register, then given her a tour of the employee areas, and made sure she'd been comfortable with how to clock in and where to put her stuff.

He'd also asked her if she wanted to get coffee sometime, but she hadn't really given him an answer. For one thing, going for coffee when she was already working the morning shift was a little tricky. Unless they went on one of her days off of course but Lucas worked all the time, so she wasn't sure how they'd coordinate that.

Or was he thinking they'd go after work? She couldn't do that either. Not with there being so much to get done at the inn.

The other thing about agreeing to go out with Lucas was that a part of her wanted to completely finalize things with Brendan. To really close that chapter of her life. Which reminded her, she needed to mail the ring back. She'd have to run by the post office tomorrow, maybe after her shift.

It would be nice to pick up a few more shifts too. The money would help. Of course on her days off, she could spend the whole day working at the inn. That would be a big help to her mom. And towards getting their dream on track.

The sooner the inn was open, the sooner their new life could begin. She wondered how long it would take to get things in good enough shape for her and her mom to move in. "Hey Travis?"

He looked over at her from the grill where he was putting the steaks on. "Yes?"

"I know you said two months to get the inn open, but when do you think the inn will be okay for residency?"

His eyes narrowed. "You mean for guests? I'm not sure I follow."

"No, I mean for my mom and me. Then we can rent this cottage out and get some money coming in."

He nodded. "Good plan. I'll be able to better answer that tomorrow, once I do my inspection and know how sound everything is." He grinned. "Hey, want to crawl under the house with me and check for termites?"

She grimaced without meaning to. "Sorry, that sounds awfully...spidery."

He laughed. "Yeah, there's a good chance of that. Don't worry, I was only teasing. If you can help me with the toilet valves in the afternoon, that's more than enough."

She grinned. "I definitely want to learn that. And any other *interior* things you want to teach me."

Her mom came back out with two glasses of pale pink wine and handed Mia one. "Here you go."

"Thanks." Mia took the glass and lifted it into the air. "Here's to new beginnings."

Her mom raised her wine while Travis raised his beer. "New beginnings," they both said. Then everyone drank a sip, sealing the toast.

Clyde meowed and went over to rub against Travis's legs. He laughed. "I think someone smells the steak."

Georgia nodded. "They do smell good. Been a while since I had a meal like this."

"Yeah?" Travis looked at her. "How come?"

Mia wondered how much her mom would tell him.

Georgia shrugged. "Things have been tight."

"I can understand that," Travis said.

"Come on, big man. Come sit with me." Mia scooped Clyde up and went back to sit in the Adirondack chair with him. As long as she was scratching him, he seemed content. Thankfully, wine only took one hand.

Travis gave her mom a little smile. "Things are on the upswing, though. You'll see."

Georgia nodded. "I believe that too. I need them to be." She sipped her wine before glancing at Mia. "Should we eat inside or out?"

"Out. It's too nice to eat inside. And look at this view."

Georgia smiled. "I couldn't agree more." She turned back to Travis. "Outside okay with you?"

"You never have to ask me that question. Outside is always okay with me." He tipped his head toward the table under the little portico. "Might want to wipe that down, though. Being this close to the sea tends to cover everything with a layer of salt and grime."

Mia carefully moved Clyde onto the seat by himself. "I'll do it." She set her wine on the deck next to the chair. "Don't you drink that, Clyde. You're not old enough."

She went inside and dug around for an old dishcloth then soaked it in hot water and went back out. Thirty seconds into wiping down the table and chairs and Travis was proven right. "A hosing down probably would have been better than being wiped off."

He nodded. "It happens. Not sure when that table was cleaned last but looks like it's been a while. That's something else that will need regular maintenance at the inn. Outdoor furniture needs constant cleaning."

"Is that why there isn't any?" Georgia asked.

"Sort of. When your aunt said she was shutting down the inn, I told her she ought to sell the deck furniture. Without being taken care of, it would be ruined after too long. So she did." He laughed softly. "That's probably the last thing she did that I told her to do."

Mia went back in, rinsed the dishcloth, then came back out for round two.

"Mia," her mom said. "You want some help?"

"No, almost done. Thanks."

Travis checked the steaks. "Good, because we're almost ready."

Georgia nodded. "I'll go get everything else together then. I still need to put the green beans in the microwave." She went in, leaving Travis and Mia by themselves.

Travis helped Mia push the chairs back in. "Your mom's had a rough go of it, huh?"

Mia nodded. "You wouldn't believe the nightmare my father's put her through." She didn't say anything else. Robert Carpenter might be her father, but her mom was the one he'd put through the most hell. It was Georgia's story to share or not.

"Oh, I think I might believe it. I have an ex-wife that could probably give him a run for his money."

"Yeah?" Mia looked up from her cleaning. "How long have you been divorced?"

"Almost a decade now."

"Wow. Long time."

He nodded. "Sometimes it is. And sometimes it isn't."

"My mom's divorce isn't final." She hoped that wasn't too much to share. "Probably soon though." She also hoped that didn't scare him off.

"I kind of figured that. Her emotions seem pretty fresh. But it's obvious how strong she is. It's not just anyone who would take on a project like the inn."

Mia smiled. "She's very strong. And smart. And a great mother."

"I could tell that from meeting you."

"Thanks." It was a sweet compliment, made even sweeter by the genuine tone of his voice. He wasn't just being nice. He was being honest.

Georgia came back out with a stack of plates, napkins and utensils on top. She stopped in front of the table but didn't put anything down. "Is it clean?"

Mia nodded. "It is now."

Georgia put the plates down. "I have to go back in for the rest."

"You need help?" Travis asked.

She shook her head. "I think you have your hands full with the steaks. But thanks." She went inside, leaving the sliding door open, returning a second later with the salad he'd

110

brought and a serving spoon. She added the bowl to the table. "Do you think I should bring out salt and pepper?"

Travis helped Mia set the table, putting his beer at the seat closest to the grill. "You seasoned the steaks, right?"

"With salt, pepper, and a little garlic powder."

"Then we should be just fine."

"All right, let me grab the green beans." She headed back in.

Travis picked up one of the plates. "Let's get those steaks off."

Mia brought the other two plates over and he added a steak to each one.

"They smell great," she said. "I'm hungrier than I thought."

"Leave some room for dessert," he said.

"Yeah? What did you bring?"

He grinned. "Chocolate silk pie."

"From Ludlows?"

He nodded. "They're kind of known for it."

"That's what Lucas told me today." He'd pointed out a few of his favorite things as he'd shown her around the store. Including the chocolate silk pie.

"Lucas Ludlow?" Travis asked.

"Yes. Do you know him? I started working at Ludlows today as a cashier. Just a few morning shifts for now, but it's a paycheck."

"That's great. I do know him. A little. Nice guy. Good family."

"Who's that?" Georgia asked as she came back out with the green beans.

"The Ludlows," Mia answered.

"That's good to hear, especially since you're working for them." She put the beans on the table. "Which chair is mine?"

"Head of the table," Mia answered.

Travis nodded. "You're the innkeeper, now. You always get head of the table."

Clyde jumped into Georgia's chair and meowed. They all laughed as she picked him up. "Maybe we should make him the honorary innkeeper."

"Sure," Mia said. "And when a customer has a complaint, they can talk to Clyde."

Chapter Fourteen

Dinner filled Georgia's stomach and her heart. The laughter and storytelling had been as wonderful as the food. Maybe part of her blissed out state was the second glass of wine, but she had a feeling it was more because she'd needed a night like this for a very long time.

Having Mia with her was an enormous blessing, despite the betrayal that had brought her daughter home.

Home, Georgia thought. That was where she was now. And why shouldn't this be home? It had been for Aunt Norma and look how well she'd done.

Georgia ate the last bite of chocolate silk pie, leaving only a few shortbread crumbs from the crust behind, and set her fork down. "I am done. That was the best meal I've had in ages. Great company, too. Good job on the steaks, Travis."

Mia nodded. "And good job on the dessert selection. I can see why Ludlows is known for that pie. Wow, is that good."

Travis grinned like a cat in the sun. "Rumor has it they use espresso powder in the chocolate to give it that extra something. Norma was constantly after Berta to recreate it for the inn."

"Hey," Georgia said. "There's a lot of pie left. You should take some home with you."

Travis's smile turned sly. "Why can't I just come back here for some?"

Mia laughed. "Yeah, mom."

Georgia held up her hands. "Or that. You are always welcome here. Or at the inn. Wherever we're living."

He put a hand on his stomach and sighed a contented sigh. "I appreciate that. And while I hate to eat and run, I have to go. I'm expecting a call at eight and I'd like to be home for it. I'd be happy to carry dishes in before I leave, though."

"Don't worry about it," Georgia said. "You cooked the steaks and brought dessert. That gets you out of clean up."

He pushed his chair back and got up. "Thank you. Thanks for the invite and the company, too. I really enjoyed it."

Georgia nodded, wondering if he'd been a little isolated since Norma had passed. Surely a man like Travis had friends. "Me, too. See you tomorrow?"

"Bright and early." He slid his chair under the table.

"How early?"

"Eight all right?"

"Perfect," Georgia said.

He gave them a nod. "Goodnight, ladies." He tilted to look under the table. "Goodnight, Clyde. If you're staying here this evening."

Clyde rolled over and showed off his belly.

Mia snorted. "I guess that answers that."

With a laugh, Travis headed for the steps, calling over his shoulder, "Enjoy the sunset."

"Night, Travis," Mia said. "We will."

He left by way of the beach.

Georgia exhaled a happy breath as she put her hands on the table. "I guess we should clean up."

"How about we don't?" Mia said. "Not just yet."

"You want to sit a little longer? Fine with me."

"No, I was thinking we could take a little walk on the beach. I mean, we live here now. We get to do that whenever we want. And I'd much rather walk on the beach than clean up dishes that can be done later. Come on, let's go. Right now."

With a smile, Georgia got out of her seat. "A walk sounds like a great idea. Especially after all that food. We'll be back in a bit, Clyde."

He didn't move.

Mia joined her and they headed down toward the water. "That pie, though, right?"

"Right. That was amazing."

They walked a little bit without saying a word, then as the sun sank lower and the sky lit up in streaks of orange and brilliant pink, Mia got her phone out.

"I have to Gram this."

Georgia's brows bent. "You have to what this?"

"Instagram, mom. Hey, you know what? I just thought of something. This place is gorgeous. And we basically own a piece of it that we can share. I'm going to start an account for the inn and let people see just what kind of paradise we have to offer."

"That sounds like a great idea, but won't that be a lot of work?"

"Not really. A picture or two a day. Maybe more when there's something good to share. And trust me, if the travel grammers find us, they'll want to come and stay. A good review from one of them and we could blow up."

"As in with business, right?"

Mia nodded. "So much you wouldn't know what to do."

"That sounds great. Just don't overwork yourself."

"I could say the same thing to you." She snapped photo after photo while they walked.

Georgia laughed. "I haven't even begun to overwork myself, but I suspect a few of those days are coming. Bound to happen with everything that needs doing."

Mia held out her phone so Georgia could see the picture. "Look at that one. I'm posting that. No need for a filter either. This place is just made for social media."

"Gorgeous." But Georgia's mind had already gone back to the inn. She prayed that Travis wouldn't discover anything majorly wrong during his inspection tomorrow. The thought of having her budget wiped out by a bad roof or wonky plumbing or hungry termites was nerve-wracking.

She did her best to shake it off and enjoy the walk. Starting tomorrow night, they might be too tired to fix their own dinner let alone walk on the beach, so she wanted to soak all of this up.

But those hard days were going to bring good days, and that was her focus. Whatever it took to get to those good days would be well worth it. The independence alone would be priceless.

She stooped to pick up another piece of beach glass, this one a dark chocolate brown, frosted with time spent tumbling in the sand and surf.

"What did you get?" Mia asked.

"Another piece of beach glass." She held it out so her daughter could see it.

"That's so pretty. Probably came from a beer bottle, huh? Kind of cool something so ordinary could produce something so interesting."

"I bet this beach is full of treasures after a storm."

"Hey," Mia said. "Let's find out after the next storm. Let's come out and see what washes up. I bet there are some amazing shells."

"Okay, I'm game. So long as it's not still pouring rain and we aren't dodging bolts of lightning." She laughed.

Mia put her phone away, then looped her arm through Georgia's. "Have you gotten a hold of Griff, yet?"

"No. To be honest, I haven't tried again. I should call him tonight when we get back in the house. I should at least tell him what's going on and where we are."

"Good idea."

She looked at her daughter. "Are you worried about your brother?"

Mia shrugged nonchalantly. "Not really. Maybe a little. Actually, it's not really worry so much as it would just be nice if he'd check in. Tell us he's okay. Stay in touch, you know? That's all."

Georgia nodded. She understood very well. "When I get him on the phone tonight, I'll let you talk to him, too."

"Thanks."

But an hour later, all Georgia could get was Griffin's voicemail. She left him a message, telling him about being in Blackbird Beach, and asking him to call as soon as he had a chance. But hanging up was hard.

She was starting to worry that something was wrong.

Or maybe that Robert had gotten to their son and somehow convinced him that Georgia was the villain in this divorce. If that was the case, Georgia worried that she might lose Griff to her soon-to-be-ex.

That wasn't a heartbreak she was prepared for.

Chapter Fifteen

Eight a.m. wasn't all that early for Georgia. Not when she'd gotten up a little after six to make sure Mia had coffee before she went off to Ludlows for her first full shift as a cashier. Mia might be an adult, but it was hard to stop mothering her daughter. Especially when they were living under the same roof.

Mia blinked sleepily. "Mom, they have coffee at the store."

"Yes, but this way you can drink a cup on the way there." Georgia smiled. There was no real argument in her daughter's voice.

"Thanks." Mia took the travel cup Georgia offered her, kissed her mom on the cheek, then went out to her car.

Georgia, still in her robe, watched her go. When Mia's car turned the corner and disappeared from view, Georgia fixed herself a cup and went outside to sit on the deck and enjoy the stillness of the morning.

Clyde, who'd slept on her bed again, went out with her. He took off toward Travis's. Maybe for breakfast. Or maybe he was just looking for a private bit of sand to do his business in. He'd yet to use the makeshift litter box. Either way,

Georgia had already decided it was time for the cat to adapt to inside life when they moved into the inn.

She couldn't bear the thought of anything happening to Aunt Norma's buddy and in a house that big, guests with cat allergies shouldn't be too affected. Still, she'd make sure people knew before they made reservations.

Had Aunt Norma done that? She made a mental note to ask Travis when she saw him. She checked the time on her phone. She still had a few minutes before she had to get ready to meet him.

Hard not to also see that there'd been no attempt by Griff to call her back. No text message either. The worry that had begun last night grew ever so slightly.

He was a grown man with his own life. She knew that. But she was still his mother. And up until a few days ago, they'd spoken on a fairly regular basis. What had happened to change that, she couldn't imagine.

Well, she could. Probably because she was a mother. And mothers had a way of running every worst-case scenario available when it came to their children. But she did her best not to do that just yet. It had only been a few days. It was very possible he'd lost his phone. Or it had been stolen.

Or he was lying hurt in a ditch somewhere, unable to— nope. She wasn't going to think like that.

She also wasn't going to think about him cutting her off because of Robert painting her as the villain in this divorce. But if that was the reason Griffin had disappeared on her, hell was going to break loose.

She would not let Robert get away with turning her son against her with his lies.

A new thought occurred to her. Maybe she should let his attorneys know how to find her. She didn't want to waste a day when it came to signing those divorce papers. She made a quick call to their offices and left a voicemail, happy not to actually have to talk to anyone.

Getting up early had its perks.

She downed the rest of her coffee and went back inside for a hot shower and some breakfast, which was two eggs over easy and toast with strawberry jam. Today was not the day to skip that meal, not when she was pretty sure she was going to burn every calorie she consumed and then some.

Half an hour later, she took the sidewalk to the inn and found Travis sitting on the porch steps, travel cup of coffee in hand. "Morning."

"Morning. I should have brought coffee with me, too. That was a good idea." At least she'd remembered her ear buds. Music would help the work go faster. It always did when she was cleaning house.

"You want to go get some? I can wait."

"Nope, I want to get to work. I can always take a break in a bit if I need it."

He stood up. He was in jeans and a T-shirt and toolbelt. There were worse things to look at first thing in the morning. "All right. The roof seems more pressing than inspecting the house for termites, so I've got the extension ladder set up on the right side of the house. I'll carry the smaller one up with me."

"Wait. You're taking another ladder up on the roof?"

He nodded. "That's the only way to access the third floor."

"Oh. Right. I hadn't really thought about that." Good thing he was here. "Do you want me to come up and hold that ladder?"

"No, that's all right. Just having you make sure the big one doesn't wobble when I come back down is all I need."

"Okay. I'm ready when you are." She followed him around the side of the house, craning her neck to see just how far up the extension ladder went. "That's high. You're really going up there?"

"No other way to inspect the roof."

"But it's...high."

He smirked. "What's the matter? You think I'm too old?"

She grinned. "I didn't say that. Especially because I think we're about the same age. But your insurance is up to date, right?"

That made him laugh. "Hey, I know I'm not as young as I used to be, but everything's in good working order and until I think otherwise, I'm not limiting what I can do."

"That's a great attitude. I'd like to think I have the same one. But I'm not going up that ladder."

"Afraid of heights?"

She shrugged one shoulder. "I wouldn't say afraid so much as I have a healthy respect for them."

"I see. Well, I promise not to take any unnecessary risks while I'm up there."

She made a face at him, enjoying the banter very much. "Was there a question that you were going to ask?"

"Just hold the ladder." Still shaking his head and smiling, he started up.

When he'd left five rungs behind, she took hold of the metal ladder, steadying it. "I wanted to ask you. What did my aunt do about having Clyde in the inn and guests who might be allergic to cats?"

"She made sure they knew ahead of time that the Sea Glass Inn was a cat-friendly property."

"Good to know. I need to make sure I do that too, then." She didn't like the idea of him doing this alone. The further up he got, the more the ladder seemed to shake.

Would he have done this if she wasn't here?

"Okay," he called to her. "I'm going to do my inspection. I'll call you when I'm ready to come down, that way you don't have to stand around and wait for me."

She nodded. "All right. I'm going to start on the yard."

He gave her a thumbs up, then went off to check the roof.

She made sure her phone wasn't on silent, then walked to the shed at the very back of the parking lot where he'd told her last night at dinner she'd find yard tools and the mower. He'd already unlocked the door, which made her wonder just how early he'd gotten here.

She got the mower out. It was the gas-powered push kind, but the grassy area of the yard wasn't that big so she had no doubts it would be sufficient. Although it was currently more jungle than yard. She wasn't sure the mower could handle it. But then Travis would have said something if he'd thought otherwise.

On the shelves in the shed, she found all kinds of tools, but the ones she was most interested in were the hedge trimmers, an edger, and a weed whacker. All seemed to be in decent shape, much like the mower. Had Travis maintained them? Something else to ask him. But then she realized he must have, if he was the one who'd taken care of the yards at both cottages. Everything there was in great shape.

Interesting that he hadn't done the inn, too. But then Aunt Norma had told him not to.

Finding someone that dedicated to a dying woman's wishes was rare.

She looked at all the tools before her, a little unsure where to start when it all desperately needed doing. Finally, she stepped out of the shed and gazed toward the roof, raising her voice a bit. "Travis?"

After a few seconds, he came to the edge of the roof. Not too close, thankfully. "Everything okay?"

She nodded. "Will this mower handle this yard?"

"It should. You going to mow?"

"Seems like the first step. It'll make everything else easier, I imagine."

"It will. Do you know how to start it?"

She took a quick look at the mower, then back at him. "I'm not sure."

"See the handle at the top? Just hold it in, then yank that cord for all you're worth. But before you do that, put your phone on vibrate because you'll never hear me call over the noise of that thing."

"Good idea. Okay, thanks."

He went back to work and she switched the mode of her phone, then put it into her back pocket again.

She held the mower handle in, like he'd said to, then yanked the string starter hard. The engine sputtered encouragingly but didn't turn over.

She tried again. Same result. A little frustrated now, she pulled the starter with everything she had.

The engine roared to life.

With a grin, she stuck her earbuds in, cranked up some tunes, and got to work. There was a little bit of yard on each side of the house, but the bulk of it was in the front. It took her about thirty-five minutes to get it all done, in part because almost all of it had to be gone over more than once. When she finished, she checked her phone to make sure she hadn't missed Travis's call.

She hadn't. She put it back on ring mode then wiped the sweat off her forehead with the back of her arm.

With the yard done, she took up the hedge trimmers next, after slipping on a pair of flowered gardening gloves. She imagined they'd belong to Norma and the thought pleased Georgia. It made her feel like her aunt was with her in some small way.

Tackling the shrubs around the house was no easy job. Ten minutes of trimming had more sweat running down her back and had only resulted in about two feet of work. Pushing the mower had been easier.

And she hadn't even begun to clean up what she was leaving behind.

Her phone rang. Had to be Travis. She got it out. "Hello?"

"I'm ready to come down."

"On my way." She'd started at the other side of the house thinking she'd work her way around by the time he was ready. That seemed laughable now. Trimmers in hand, she walked back and found him staring down at her from the second story.

She put the trimmers on the ground and took hold of the ladder, her heart just slightly in her throat at the thought of his descent. "Got it," she called up.

He gave her a nod, then took hold of the part of the ladder that jutted beyond the roof line, swung his leg around, planted it on the closest rung and climbed down.

She realized when he had about three feet left to go that every muscle in her body was tensed. She relaxed as he touched solid ground. She laughed softly. "I'm glad you're down. I didn't like that."

"Holding the ladder?"

"You being up so high. I know you were careful, but it was still unsettling."

He smiled. "I promise, I was fine."

She nodded, knowing he probably thought her fear was silly. She changed the subject. "So? What's the verdict?"

He stopped smiling. "There's a section of roof that needs to be replaced. I'll have to get some plywood, felt, and shingles, but I can get it done in a day. Well, by tomorrow anyway. Thankfully, that's the only section I found that needs to be repaired."

"Wait. You can do it yourself?"

"Yes. If the whole roof had to be replaced, you'd need a roofing contractor, but I can handle this. Couple hundred bucks, tops." He stared up at the roof. "Kind of surprised there wasn't more damage."

Relief swept through her and without thinking about it, she let out a shriek of joy and hugged him.

The moment her arms were around him, she realized what she was doing and she let him go.

He was smiling.

She was mortified. "I didn't mean...I was just...I shouldn't have done that." She took a breath, doing her best not to think about how warm and nice he'd felt.

He nodded, grinning like he'd won something. "You're welcome."

Maggie Miller

Chapter Sixteen

With her Hall and Oates playlist blaring, Georgia spent the rest of the morning on the yard with her head down and her mind focused on her work. At least she hoped that's what Travis thought she was doing. She did *not* want him to know where her mind really was.

On him. And how nice it had been to hug him, to feel that connection with a man again. Especially a male someone. And how different he felt than Robert.

Robert's idea of sports was watching them on TV. As a result, he resembled the couch more than he did the players.

Whereas Travis was more like one of the players. He was hard and lean, and she couldn't remember the last time she'd been that close to a body like his. Except for maybe her son and that wasn't even comparable.

To complicate matters, hugging Travis had only brought back to mind what he'd looked like when she'd first met him. Wearing nothing but a towel.

She would have been sweating even without the work she was doing.

Despite her thoughts, she was able to accomplish a lot. She managed to trim all the hedges around the house. Now she was working on raking up all the pieces and putting them in yard waste bags so they could be picked up.

She should ask Travis what day pick up was or if they'd have to haul the stuff off themselves, but that would mean talking to him. Which she'd have to do eventually, she knew that, but she just wasn't quite ready.

Besides, she didn't know exactly where he was. He might have been inside. Or under the house, which he'd mentioned. Or back on the roof. Wouldn't he have asked her to hold the ladder again, though?

A hand touched her shoulder and she jumped, yanking out her ear buds as she reacted.

Travis stood behind her, smiling. He was wearing a white paper jumpsuit that was pretty filthy. "Sorry. Didn't mean to scare you."

"It's okay. I just didn't hear you. I had my music on."

He nodded. "Sounds like Hall and Oates."

"It is."

"Good stuff. I was just under the house. No sign of termites, so we're in good shape there."

"That's fantastic." She held tight to the rake. She did not need to hug him a second time. Even though the idea had its appeal.

"It is." He hooked his thumb toward his truck. "I'm going to the hardware store to get a few things. Since this is officially for the inn, how do you want to handle the bills?"

She didn't want him paying for things. "I hadn't thought about that. I guess I need to start a business account and get a credit card. Or a checkbook."

"Are you sure there isn't one already?"

She thought about that a minute. "No. But why would there be?"

"Because your aunt did things like that. The lawyer would have said something about it, most likely."

"He did give me a packet of stuff. Which I still haven't gone through." She really needed to do that. "I'd better go check."

"All right. In the meantime, I can work on the raking."

That reminded her to ask about the pick up time. "Will they come and get yard waste, or do we have to haul it?"

"They'll pick it up, but it has to be bagged or in cans and nothing larger than six feet long."

She looked at the shrub scraps. "I think we're good so far then."

"We are."

"Okay, I'll run back to the cottage and check on that account. If I don't see anything, I'll call Mr. Gillum."

"I'll be here." He took the rake from her and got to work.

She headed down the sidewalk. That interaction hadn't been bad. Having something important to talk about, like money, had helped.

Or maybe she was just imagining the chemistry between them. After all, she'd been married for thirty-one years. It was very possible she'd forgotten what real chemistry was. The spark between her and Robert hadn't gone completely out until she'd found out about his cheating, but it had died down to a dull ember years before.

She shook her head. She didn't want to think about all of that again. After she'd found out he was cheating, she'd blamed him, then blamed herself for not keeping things alive between them.

But she knew better now. Sure, she'd gained a little weight. Having kids did that. But so did life. And putting everyone else ahead of her own needs. It also wasn't her job to keep her husband faithful. He'd promised that the day they'd gotten married.

And if they were going to compare who'd taken better care of themselves, Robert hadn't exactly shied away from the beer and snacks. He'd easily gained fifty pounds since their wedding day.

Sure, he liked to pat his belly and compliment her cooking, but that was only cute for so long. It was just an excuse.

She blew out a long breath. Enough of that. Her marriage to Robert was over and her new life, her new Blackbird Beach life, had begun.

And if that meant a little flirting with Travis, there was nothing wrong with that. Who cared if she'd hugged him? He certainly didn't seem to be hung up about it.

She went into her cottage and straight for the packet Mr. Gillum had given her, which she'd left on her nightstand with the intention of looking through it. After failing to reach Griffin, however, she hadn't been in the mood.

She opened the flap and dumped everything onto the bed. A checkbook was one of the first things to fall out. With a smile, she picked it up and took a better look at it. Her name was printed on the checks, along with the Sea Glass Inn.

Aunt Norma sure had been confident about what Georgia was going to do. It made Georgia smile. This was a clear sign she was doing the right thing.

Just to be sure the checkbook was okay to use, she took out her phone and called Mr. Gillum.

She asked for him when the receptionist answered and was immediately transferred.

"Ms. Carpenter, good afternoon. What can I do for you?"

"Hi, Mr. Gillum. I was wondering about the checkbook in the packet of stuff you left me. Is that ready to go or do I need to do anything to activate it?"

"It's ready to use, although the bank would like you to come in and sign a new signature card when you get a chance. I've given them all the paperwork they needed to confirm the account, however."

"Okay, great."

"The credit card won't need any other signatures as that comes back to your aunt's account. You're on that one as a secondary signer."

"There's a credit card?" She looked around in the paperwork and found a small manilla envelope. As soon as she picked it up, she could tell there was a card inside. "Wait, I found it. That's okay to use as well?"

"Yes."

"That's great. The roof of the inn needs to be repaired so this is just perfect."

"I'm glad to hear work has begun."

"Yep, Travis and I started this morning."

"You'll need to apply for a new operating license, but I can handle that for you, if you'd like."

"Fantastic, thank you, go right ahead. One more thing. Can Travis use this credit card for supplies, or do I need to go with him?"

"If he's going to Beachside Hardware, I'm guessing he'd be all right to use it. They know him. And they knew your aunt. Couldn't hurt for you to go along once, though. Just to let them know you're the new owner."

"Okay, maybe I should do that then." Not that spending more time with Travis was such a hardship.

"If there's anything else I can help you with, don't hesitate to call."

"Thanks. I'll do that. Have a good day."

"You too." He hung up.

Georgia tore the little envelope open and dumped out the credit card. She glanced at it, then grinned. "Thank you, once again, Aunt Norma."

She tucked it into her back pocket and returned to the inn. Travis had gotten most of the shrub debris raked up and binned. He'd also taken off the dirty white paper jumpsuit. "You work fast."

He smiled. "Years of practice, I suppose."

"I have a credit card and a checking account. But Mr. Gillum said I should probably go with you to Beachside Hardware, just to let them know I'm good with you using the card in the future."

"Wouldn't hurt to meet Alan, either."

"Alan?"

"He's the owner. Alan Crenshaw. He knew your aunt, too. I'm sure he'd be pleased to meet you and know the inn was staying in the family."

"Okay. Should we get cleaned up?" They were both sweaty and a little grimy.

He laughed. "It's a hardware store. Based on what they're used to, we're dressed for the prom."

She crossed her arms. "You went to a very different prom than I did." Then she smiled. "But I know what you mean."

"Let me put a few of these things away and we can go."

A couple minutes later, they were in his truck and off to the hardware store. It was near the edge of town, by the Frosty King, a soft-serve ice cream place.

"Hey." She pointed at the little drive-up hut with the big ice cream cone on top as they went by. "I remember the Frosty King from when I was a kid. Nice to see it's still here."

"Best homemade soft serve around." He parked in the Beachside Hardware lot and they got out. "They make regular ice cream too now. All homemade. You can't beat 'em."

He grabbed a long, low flatbed kind of cart and led her back to the end of the store where she felt very much like a stranger in a strange land. Lengths of lumber filled the shelves and not too far away a man was running a saw, cutting some of that timber to length for a customer.

"Do we need a lot of stuff?" she asked.

"Nothing outside of what I need to fix the roof. Unless there's something else you can think of?"

"Cleaning supplies. I saw some in the pantry at the inn, but I'm not sure it's going to be enough for the job we have to tackle."

"If you want to grab some while we're here, go ahead. It's going to take me a bit to pull everything I need."

"All right. I'll find you when I'm done." She followed the signs hanging from the ceiling to the cleaning supplies area, grabbing a basket on her way. She was just about to add a jug of window cleaner when her phone rang with an incoming call from Mia.

"Hi there."

"Hey, where are you guys? I just got home from work."

"Hardware store getting stuff to fix the roof. We shouldn't be too long."

"Okay, I'll have lunch then be ready to go when you get back."

"Sounds good. How was your first full day?"

"Nice," Mia said with a smile in her voice. "Busy. And fried chicken was on sale so I brought a box home."

"That sounds great. I might have some for lunch myself when we get back." But Georgia had a feeling fried chicken wasn't the real reason Mia sounded so happy.

Chapter Seventeen

Mia hung up, changed out of her work clothes and into shorts and an old T-shirt, then ate a piece of fried chicken standing over the sink. Not her favorite way to eat a meal, but she was eager to get to work at the inn. The idea of being part of something like that just thrilled her.

Almost as much as working with Lucas.

She grinned as she took another bite. He'd mentioned going for coffee again. And she'd almost said yes. At least today, she'd remembered to go to the post office and mail her engagement ring back.

Sending it insured had been expensive, but it was money well spent. She was completely free from Brendan now. Hopefully he'd stop calling, too. Now, if she wanted to say yes to coffee with Lucas, she could without any guilt or strings attached.

She just might, too. In a couple weeks, after she got to know him a little better. There was no reason to rush things.

The fried chicken was delicious. And gone. She tossed the bones in the trash, then helped herself to a slice of the chocolate silk pie left over from last night's dinner. She ate that standing over the sink, too, holding it like a slice of pizza and supporting the crust with her fingers. No dirty dishes that way.

The pie was just as amazing as she remembered. She'd tried to get Lucas to tell her what made it so good, but he'd just smiled and said, "Family secret."

Maybe someday he'd tell her. Or maybe the next cook at the inn would figure it out.

She finished up the pie, washed her hands, then headed to the inn. Her mom and Travis were still gone, so she looked around to see what needed doing next. Travis was going to teach her to change out the toilet valves when he got back, but she couldn't even think about working on those without him.

Someone, probably her mom, had done an outstanding job of getting the yard in shape. It wasn't done, but it was certainly looking a lot better. All of the planted beds were still filled with weeds, however. Maybe she'd work on those. She found a pair of flowered gardening gloves on the porch steps. Her mom must have had them on.

She grabbed them, went to the first bed, and got to work. A couple minutes in, she realized she should have brought her airpods so she could listen to music. Also, she was sweating like crazy. But she hadn't thought this was going to be easy.

And as soon as her mom and Travis got back, Mia would be headed inside to work. On toilets. She laughed. How much had her life changed?

It was easily another forty minutes before they returned, however, and by then, Mia had just about finished the first bed. Well, she'd done about two thirds of it. The weeds seemed to pop back up whenever she looked away. She got to her feet, brushing off her knees, and went to greet them, taking off the gardening gloves as she went. "Need help?"

"Sure," Travis said. "There's lots to carry in." He handed her a couple bags. "Toilet valves. And some other supplies."

She took it. "I'm ready to learn."

"Good, because those really need doing and if you can handle them, I'll be able to get started on the roof."

Georgia got out of the truck with two bags of cleaning supplies. "You're going to do that today?"

"The sooner the better. That leak is only going to get worse." He tilted his head slightly, a curious expression coming over his face. "I'll be fine."

"You'd better call me when you need me to hold the ladder."

"I will. Promise."

Mia wasn't sure what all of that was about, but she carried the bags she'd been given to the porch. She put the gloves back on the step where she'd found them.

Her mom came along with her own bags. "How was work?"

"Good. So was the fried chicken I brought home. You should have some for lunch. I did."

But her mother wasn't letting up that easily. "Just good?"

Mia couldn't help but smile. "What are you getting at?"

"Nothing. Just making conversation. Chicken sounds great." Georgia looked at the flower bed by the fence where some of the crepe myrtles were planted. "You got a good start on those weeds. Thanks."

"Sure. I wanted to do something while I waited."

Travis carried some lumber from the back of the truck and leaned it against the side of the house. Then he jogged up onto the porch and grabbed the bag of toilet valves. "All right, let's go have a little plumbing lesson."

"Don't we need tools?" Mia asked.

"There's a toolbox inside. It belongs to the inn so I figured we'd use that one so you can be comfortable with where it is and what the tools in it are for."

She rubbed her hands together and looked at her mom. "Wish me luck."

"You won't need it," Georgia said as she slipped the gardening gloves back on. "You have a good teacher."

Travis smiled at her, then held the door for Mia. "After you."

She went in, happy to be in cooler air. "Did you crank the AC a little? Feels cooler in here."

"I did, but it's still not as cool as it should be. We'll have to get the HVAC guys out to do an inspection."

"Is that going to be expensive?"

"All depends on what the system needs." He pointed toward the kitchen. "Toolbox is in the pantry. Let's grab it, then we'll start with the powder room down here and if that goes well, you can take over."

Mia made a little face. "You think I can get the hang of it that fast?"

"Changing out a toilet valve is pretty easy. And you made it through college. If you can do that, you should be able to do this."

"Okay." But college was more books than bathrooms.

They got the toolbox and he set things up in the powder room, taking off the top of the toilet tank and pointing out the various parts.

"You hear how the water never stops trickling?"

She listened, then nodded.

"There could be a few reasons for that. One is that the fill valve isn't properly adjusted, but that's not the case here. These toilets have sat too long without being flushed, allowing the flapper valve to get corroded. That stops it from sealing properly. Once it's changed, that trickling will stop." He walked her through the steps, then went over them all once more before he actually did anything. "Now. What's the first thing we do?"

"Turn the water off," Mia answered. He'd made that pretty clear.

"Yep. Go ahead and do it."

She crouched down to access the valve and cranked it off. "Do you know the Ludlows?"

"I know of them."

Water off, she stood up. "How's that?"

"Perfect. Now what's next?"

"Detach the old flapper valve?"

"Yep. Go ahead."

She got to work on that. "What do you know about Lucas Ludlow?"

"Seems like a nice kid." Travis watched her. "That's right, just pop it off those little prongs. Why do you ask? Are you having trouble with him?"

"Oh no, nothing like that." She held up the flapper valve, now free. "Ta da!"

Travis smiled. "Toilets aren't all that complicated, are they?"

"They really aren't. Which is like a lesson in itself." She put the old valve down and dug a new one out of the bag. "He seems nice. He asked me out for coffee."

"I see. And you want to know what kind of guy he is before you say yes."

"Sort of. I'm not sure I'm ready for a date with him just yet. Just curious about him I guess." She glanced at Travis. "I just hook this one on where the old one was?"

"You might want to check the opening first. Make sure it doesn't need to be cleaned off, but if there's no build up on it, then go ahead and attach the new one."

She ran her hand around the plastic ring inside the tank. "Seems okay."

"Put the new valve on then."

She took the valve out of the package and started hooking it onto the prongs that allowed it to hinge up and down.

"That's smart to ask about him," Travis said. "I've never heard anything bad about him. He was on the high school football team. I remember that. There was some talk about him getting a big scholarship, but he blew his knee out and that was that. Went to a local community college, then straight to work for his father."

She nodded. The new flapper was slicker than the old one. She almost had it attached twice but it had slipped off the prongs right at the last second.

Travis leaned against the wall, still watching. "He'll inherit that store someday, I imagine. I suppose that makes him a pretty good catch."

She looked up through her bangs at Travis. "I don't care about that. I just want a nice guy. My last was..." She sighed. "Never mind. He's not worth it." She didn't want to talk about Brendan. She was afraid she'd get mad and emotional and cry.

She did not want to cry in front of Travis. Not while he was teaching her to fix toilets. She didn't want him to think she was some weak, emotional woman and shy away from teaching her to do other things. Although he didn't seem like the kind to react that way.

"It's okay," he said. "I'm not going to judge you one way or the other. I know how life can go sideways when you least expect it. And how people can disappoint you. Especially the ones who shouldn't."

Had he read her mind? She got the flapper on. She straightened and smiled triumphantly. "There. How was that?"

He looked into the tank. "Looks perfect. Now just reattach the chain and we'll give it a test flush."

She did that, then put her hand on the handle. "Okay?"

"Are you sure there's nothing else you're supposed to do?"

She thought for a moment, then smiled. "Turn the water back on?"

He nodded. "That's it."

She did that, then flushed the toilet. The water whooshed away and the tank refilled and that was it.

Travis nodded his head. "You're a good student and a fast learner. Well done."

"That's it? I did it?"

"You did it. All by yourself. I just told you what to do."

"Wow." She grinned and felt like she could take on the world. "I can't believe I just fixed a toilet. Thank you for teaching me that. I hope there's some other stuff I can learn."

He looked as pleased as she felt. "I will teach you anything you want to learn. And around here, there's a pretty long list. Nothing on the roof, though. I don't think your mom would like that and I'd rather stay on her good side."

"I don't blame you. I don't think I'm cut out for anything involving heights anyway." She hesitated as she gathered up the tools. "You like my mom, don't you?"

"I think she's a very nice person."

That wasn't what Mia had meant, but his smile said more than his words. "She thinks you're a very nice person too."

He laughed softly. "Good to know. You feel like you can do the rest of the flapper valves on your own?"

She gave it two seconds of thought. "Yeah, I can do it. And if I get hung up, I'll come get you."

"Except I'm going to be on the roof."

"Oh. Right. Well, if I get hung up, I'll just wait then."

He nodded. "Good plan. Just don't forget the first step."

"Turn the water off. And then of course, back on."

"That's it. You've got it. You're going to do fine. You'll be replacing fixtures before you know it."

"Thanks." Did he mean putting in new faucets? Because that seemed a lot more complicated. But his faith in her was encouraging.

It also left her a little angry at her own father. Travis had just spent more time with her than her own father had in the last year. And had a more meaningful conversation.

Not hard to see why her mom liked Travis. Not hard at all.

Chapter Eighteen

Georgia held the ladder while Travis carried his tools and supplies up to the roof. The thought of him up there again, this time with power tools, was a little nerve-wracking.

Obviously, he knew what he was doing.

But that didn't stop all the worry. Funny to think she could entertain such emotions toward a man she'd just met, but Travis was so easy to like, which made him easy to care about. And not just because he was such an important part of getting the inn back up and running.

He was, in a lot of ways, her last connection to Norma. She was glad when he came down the ladder again. "Are you done?"

He climbed off the ladder and shook his head. "Done taking my supplies up. I haven't even started the repair yet. Just wanted to get everything up there. Now, I'm going to eat some lunch. You should probably do the same. Working like this can build up a powerful appetite. Make sure to drink plenty of water too. You don't want to get dehydrated."

"Right. Hey, Mia brought some fried chicken home from Ludlows. You want to come over for that? And some pie? I figure since we're burning all these calories. I can also offer you an unending supply of delicious Blackbird Beach tap water."

He laughed. "Okay, sounds good. Thanks."

They walked to her cottage. As soon as they were inside, she went to the kitchen sink to wash up. He waited beside her to do the same.

She dried her hands on a towel, then dug around in the fridge. She found the box of chicken, a container of potato salad, a half a jar of bread and butter pickles, and the chocolate silk pie. She got them all out, along with plates and utensils and put it all on the table. She filled two glasses with ice and water and brought them to the table as well.

"Fancy lunch," Travis said. He dried his hands on the same towel she'd used. "More like a picnic."

Georgia laughed. "This isn't fancy. And if it was a picnic, I'd expect wine."

He laughed as he sat across from her. "It's fancy compared to the cheese and bologna on wheat I'd usually have on a big workday. I hope I don't need a nap afterwards."

She shrugged as she took her seat. "You can always do the roof tomorrow."

"Maybe. But if another storm rolls in, I'll be wishing I'd already taken care of it."

"True," she said. She took a piece of chicken, then spooned some potato salad onto her plate and stabbed her fork into a few pickles. "Are we expecting bad weather?"

"Not that I've heard, but around here, you never really know."

She nodded. That was true about most parts of Florida. It could rain on one side of the street but not the other. "I guess that too, the sooner the repair is done the less damage there will be to fix."

"Exactly. Once I get the roof done, I'll look at the ceiling inside. Not sure if that will need replacing or just repainting. Either way, I'll get it done."

"I know you will." She took a bite of chicken, swallowing before she spoke again. "That reminds me, how did Mia do with the plumbing lesson?"

"She did great." He had a forkful of potato salad in one hand. "She's a smart girl. She might end up taking over my job."

"Oh, no, I can't have that," Georgia said. "I need her brain to help me run the place. She went to school for hotel restaurant management. I don't have the first clue about the business side of things. Without her, I'm sunk. Not to mention, it would be nice to see her put that degree to work."

He finished his bite of food before speaking. "Norma never went to school for it, you know."

"Then how did she figure it out? Running an inn isn't exactly easy."

He shrugged. "She just...did. She had a knack for it, I guess. I suppose it helped that people loved her. And if they didn't actually love her, they were smart enough to maintain a healthy respect. Bottom line, she was pretty good about knowing who to soothe and who to send packing."

Georgia nodded, thinking about her aunt. "She definitely had a certain effect on people. I don't think I'm quite that kind of person, though."

His gaze held a lot of amusement.

"What?"

He gestured with a half-eaten drumstick. "You undersell yourself."

Did she? She thought about that for a few seconds before answering. "Maybe I do. I don't mean to. I think that comes from…" How much was she willing to share? "My soon-to-be-ex wasn't the most complimentary of men. Over the years, that took its toll. Not using that as an excuse, really, but getting over the consequences of my marriage is probably going to take some time."

He nodded with great compassion. "I can understand that."

"You were married?"

"I was." His gaze was on his plate.

"Do you have any kids?"

His pause was a lot longer this time and he didn't answer until he'd let out a low, slow breath. "I have a daughter."

"Oh, that's nice. How old is she?"

"Twenty-six."

"A few years older than Mia." Might be nice for Mia to get to know another young woman in the area. "Does she live around here?"

"No. She lives in Alabama near her mother."

Georgia got the sense this wasn't the most comfortable of topics for him, but her curiosity had been activated and she couldn't help but ask one more question before letting it go. "Do you get to see her much?"

He stared at his plate again and she instantly regretted the question. She shouldn't have pried. Too late now.

He exhaled as though the world weighed on him. "I haven't seen her since she was seventeen. That was also the first and last time I saw my grandson."

Georgia's mouth fell open. "You have a grandson?" He'd said his daughter had been seventeen. She'd had the baby pretty early then.

He continued to stare at his plate. "I do. Clayton. He's nine. Likes football and NASCAR and that's about all I know about him." Travis looked up, the abject misery on his face as plain as could be.

"I'm sorry," she said quietly, feeling like she'd really stepped in it. "I didn't mean to be so nosy about something so sensitive."

"No, it's okay. It's nice to talk about him, actually." He sipped his water. "Samantha, that's my daughter, she got pregnant in high school. The boyfriend's parents wanted her to get rid of it. So did my wife. Then Jillian, my wife, she decided Sam should have the baby but put it up for adoption."

He shook his head, swallowing like it was an effort. "Her own grandchild. Can you imagine?"

Georgia couldn't. Having your first grandchild put up for adoption sounded like a nightmare. There were no words.

Travis continued. "I was the only one who stood by Sam's decision to have the baby and keep it. Eventually my wife came around, but too much damage had been done. It broke us up. Although, truth be told, I think Jillian had wanted out for some time. She thought life owed her more, you might say. At least more than the life I was able to give her."

"Wow." Georgia felt a little dumbstruck by his revelation. Not to mention, deeply sympathetic. She couldn't imagine the hurt he'd felt because of this situation. And continued to feel. From what his wife had done, of course. But to have a grandchild you didn't get to see? That was terrible. She put her fork down. "I'm really sorry."

"Me too."

"And now you don't get to see him?"

"I've only seen him that one time in person. Now I just have to stalk my ex-wife and daughter's Facebook pages for a glimpse of him."

"That's not fair. He should know his grandfather." She wanted to ask more questions, but she'd pried enough. If he wanted to share, he would. His decision.

"I hope he figures that out. I send him a birthday gift every year, but I don't know if he gets it or not."

"Oh, Travis. That's heartbreaking."

He smiled, but it was a tense expression meant to offer the lie that it was all okay. Hard to pull off when they both knew it wasn't. "I didn't mean to ruin lunch."

"You didn't. Not even a little. I feel honored that you shared all that with me. I'm sure it wasn't easy."

"Thanks." His smile relaxed a bit. "Actually, I feel better that I told you. Which I didn't expect to happen."

"Good. I'm glad about that." Why she'd ever questioned her decision to share with him, she had no idea. He was clearly a man who understood just how awful people could be. "If you ever want to talk about anything, my door is always open. Talking is good. I mean, we all have our baggage, right? Sharing makes the burden lighter."

"I suppose we do. And you're right, talking is good." His smile softened further. "That's why I make myself available every night at eight. I've always told Sam if she wants to talk, I'm available then."

"But she's never called, has she?"

He shook his head. "Not yet." His smile was gone again. "Not yet."

Maggie Miller

Chapter Nineteen

By the third flapper valve, Mia felt like a pro. She hummed a little while she worked, sang some, too, but mostly thought about everything she'd learned in school.

Not one class had covered flapper valve replacement, making her wonder if any of her studies were going to be that useful in the actual running of an inn. Hopefully, they would be, but clearly there was a lot that had been left out, too.

Like all the practical, hands on stuff. She had half a mind to ask for some of her parents' tuition money back. Not that it would do any good.

Didn't really matter now, because she was going to make this inn successful if it took every brain cell in her head.

Last night before going to bed, she'd started a new Instagram account for the inn. Tonight she planned on getting another shot of the sunset to add to it. And if she timed her morning right, she could probably catch the sunrise, too.

She thought about what else she wanted to highlight on the new account. More pictures of the beach, definitely. Possibly pictures of the town. Some of the shops, maybe. But should she capture the progress of what they were doing now? Would that get people interested in visiting when they finally opened up to paying guests?

She leaned back, thinking about that. People might get invested in the place if they could see it being brought back to life and get a feel for all the work and love going into it. People loved fixer-upper TV shows. How was this any different?

Impulsively, she took out her phone and snapped a picture of the new valve she'd just installed.

Okay, flapper valves might not make for the best gram post ever, but wouldn't future guests want to know that no detail was too small? Or was toilet repair a bridge too far? Hard to know. Stranger things had been posted on social media, that was for sure.

Mia decided to talk to her mom about it and see what she thought. She also wanted to scope out other inns and beach front B&Bs to see what kinds of stuff they were gramming. Then she'd decide how personal to make the account.

She got back to work and in short time, had all the valves replaced, finishing up the one on the third floor to the sounds of Travis running a saw on the roof. It reminded her of a dentist's drill but on steroids.

Not the most pleasant of sounds.

After gathering her things, she headed back downstairs. She put the toolbox back in the pantry, then walked out into the living room and took a long look around, imagining the inn filled with guests.

Her mouth curved into a smile. It was going to be amazing. Who wouldn't love this place? And she and her mom were going to make it spectacular. The saw started up again. With Travis's help, naturally.

Without him, they'd be in a really tough spot. They'd have to hire someone and finding someone who was good at their job and trustworthy wasn't always the easiest thing. She worried too, that without him, an unscrupulous contractor might try to take advantage of them.

Another benefit of having Travis around was him protecting them from that.

Besides that, Travis was a nice guy. Who had a vested interest in seeing the inn back up and running. That alone was a tremendous check in his favor.

Aunt Norma had done a good thing when she'd hired him. But she'd probably known what she was doing. Everything Mia's mom had told her about Aunt Norma made it seem like the woman had been one smart, tough cookie.

Mia wondered if anyone would ever think that about her. Maybe Brendan would, after he got the ring back and realized she wasn't going to settle for someone who didn't love her enough to be faithful.

His loss. Clearly. She wondered if he'd end up with Sarah. Not that she cared. They could have each other. Although she really wished she could call him up and tell him she'd just changed a houseful of flapper valves. He probably didn't even know what a flapper valve was let alone how to change one.

Mia headed outside. She was definitely leveling up. And leaving that loser behind was just the beginning.

She found her mom raking up more shrub clippings at the back of the house. Apparently, they'd both forgotten there were some bushes back there, too. "Wow, the hedges look great. I can't believe you did all that."

"Thanks." Georgia stopped, leaning on the rake. "It really does make a difference, doesn't it? With them done and the yard mowed, the place looks a hundred times better."

Mia looked around. "It really does. What can I help with?"

"You already got those flapper valves done?"

Mia smiled proudly. "I did."

"You are amazing. I am so impressed with you."

"Be impressed with Travis. He's the one who taught me."

Georgia grinned. "How about I be impressed with both of you? And if you want to help, there's always more weeding to do. Or cleaning to be done inside. In fact…you could start by cleaning out that fridge."

Mia grimaced. "Yeah, okay."

Georgia hesitated. "Maybe have a look at the ovens, too. I bet they need to be cleaned. If they have a self-cleaning function, we should probably set that."

Mia put her hands on her hips. "I know less about self-cleaning ovens than I did about flapper valves. This sounds like something else I'm going to need a lesson in."

"Don't worry about the ovens. I think the fridge will keep you busy for the rest of the day."

Mia nodded. "All right. You know, if I do finish early, I might start on the pantry. I bet a lot of that food is expired or stale. No point in keeping any of that."

"Good plan." Georgia started raking again. "Let me know if you need help."

"Will do, but I think I'll be all right. Unless something in the fridge has grown legs and decides to attack." Mia walked back to the porch, laughing.

She went straight to the kitchen, found the trash can, then dug around in the pantry for a liner. Once that was set up, she took a breath and opened the fridge.

It was surprisingly clean. And what food was in there was mostly jarred stuff like pickles and jam and mayo.

Didn't matter. It was all going, including the couple of Styrofoam containers that she was not going to be opening. Probably leftovers or takeout food. Either way, it didn't need to be examined for her to decide what to do with it.

She emptied everything into the trash, then wiped down all the shelves and drawers. Aunt Norma had kept a pretty tidy place. Mia knew she needed to be better about that herself. Especially when she was living here.

It wouldn't do to leave a mess around with guests at the inn.

With the fridge done, she tackled the freezer. Couple pints of old ice cream, lots and lots of unidentifiable foil-wrapped things, a box of broccoli that was pretty much a brick of ice, and another couple of TV dinners. All of that went into the bin as well.

But then, in the back, Mia found a small-ish box wrapped heavily in foil. It was perfectly square and had some weight, but not enough to feel like steaks or stew or something hearty.

Curiosity got the best of her. She pulled it out and peeled back a few layers of foil trying to figure out what was in it. Underneath the layers of foil were several more layers of plastic wrap, and beneath that was a simple clear bakery box.

In an instant, the realization of what she was looking at hit her.

The top tier of Aunt Norma's wedding cake saved for a first anniversary that never happened.

Her mom had told her all about Cecil and Norma, and how he'd passed away right after their honeymoon.

It was sweet and sad, and Mia felt like she'd just shared a moment with the great aunt she'd only barely known. Ivory icing decorated the little round cake with graceful swoops and delicate swirls that were accented with clusters of tiny roses. The whole thing was lovely. "Oh, Aunt Norma. I'm so sorry you never got to share this with Cecil."

Mia carefully wrapped the cake back up and returned it to the freezer. She wasn't sure what to do with it, but it certainly wasn't going into the trash.

She tied up the liner bag and hauled it outside, setting it near the gate before going to see where the actual trash can was. She went through the breakfast room to the little entry foyer on the side of the house that led out to the parking lot.

She found the can with several other cans behind a wooden screen. She tossed the bag into one then hauled it to the curb, hoping the can wouldn't sit there for too long, then went to find her mother.

As she walked across the yard, she stopped to look at the property again. It really was coming along even with the few small things that had been done. More than ever now she wanted to make Aunt Norma proud.

The image of the cake stayed in her head.

There had to be a way to preserve it, but more than that, it felt like a sign from Norma herself. Mia shook her head.

She'd never been one to go in for such things as signs but finding that cake had started wheels turning.

A new thought came to her. A way to maybe celebrate Aunt Norma and bring some interest to the inn. But it was just the beginning of a thought. She'd sit on it a while and let it bloom a bit before she mentioned it.

Plus she'd have to do a little homework and see if such a thing even made sense. And if it was possible. It might be more of an undertaking than they could handle.

Unless she had help.

Maggie Miller

Chapter Twenty

Georgia hadn't had such a long, hard, rewarding day in many, many years. She stood under the spray of hot water, thankful the cottage had such good water pressure.

Without a hot shower after a day like that, she wasn't sure she'd make it.

They'd called it quits about an hour before sunset. Travis hadn't quite finished the roof, but he'd put a tarp in place just in case of rain. Mia said she'd made great progress in the kitchen and Georgia had wrestled about half of the landscaping into submission. Okay, maybe a third of it. Or a fourth, considering she'd uncovered a few more flower beds than she'd originally thought existed. But she'd made a great start.

With all of that accomplished, they'd retreated to their cottages to shower, recover, and refuel. They'd probably all fall into bed before their usual times, too. At least Georgia figured she would. She was so tired she wasn't sure she'd even have the energy to read more than a chapter or two of her current book.

She kept a good thought for Travis, that tonight would be the night his daughter called. Maybe tonight would be the night Griffin called, too.

Georgia finally got out of the shower, wrapped her hair in a towel and her body in a robe, and went out to the kitchen. Mia, who'd showered first, was sitting at the kitchen table scrolling through her phone.

"You want a glass of wine?" Georgia asked.

"Sure," Mia said. "I'm about to go snap some sunset pics."

Georgia stopped in her tracks, thinking. "That gives me an idea."

"About?"

"Your brother. Maybe I'll text him a picture of the beach. You know, just a casual wish you were here kind of thing. What do you think?"

Mia shrugged. "I think anything's worth a shot." She got up. "I'm going out to get my sunset photos. How about I meet you on the deck after?"

"Sounds good. I'll throw some clothes on."

"Oh, one more thing," Mia said. "Clyde's probably ready for dinner. I brought a few cans of cat food home from Ludlows today. Nothing fancy, just the stuff they had on sale. And yes, I used my employee discount. The food is on the counter there."

"Okay, I'll take our wine and his dinner out to the deck and you can join me when you're done taking pictures."

"Cool." Mia headed outside.

Georgia poured one glass of pinot for herself, had a few sips, then went back to her bedroom and put on some yoga pants and a T-shirt. She was going to be sore tomorrow, she just knew it, but nothing a few Advil wouldn't fix.

And there was too much to be done to take a day off. Especially when she was only going to get sore again. She smiled. It was a good kind of sore, though. The kind earned by doing hard work.

Nothing wrong with that.

Before long, she'd be used to it. She looked forward to that day. Owning her own business had been a dream she'd never really thought obtainable until now.

Dressed, she returned to the kitchen, had another sip of wine, then fixed Clyde a dish of food and took it outside.

He was in his usual spot under the table.

"Hungry, big man?"

He came trotting over and started in on the bowl immediately.

She watched him eat, admiring the beautiful shades of orange in his coat. "You don't know it yet, but you're about to become an indoor cat. Back in your old house."

But sadly, not with his old owner. She hoped Aunt Norma knew they were taking care of him.

Georgia went back inside for the two glasses of wine. When she returned to the deck, she put a glass by each chair, then took a photo of the beach and the water to send to Griff. She sat down, typed out a quick note with the picture and sent it on its way.

With that done, she settled back into the Adirondack chair, hoping to hear the familiar ding of a return text before long.

Mia stood down by the water's edge, tipping her phone back and forth as she took photos. She looked beautiful in the glow of sunset.

Georgia was so proud of her. Mia had really stepped up, putting her heartache on the backburner to throw herself into this new life. Maybe all the work was helping her get over Brendan and Sarah. Or maybe Mia was just more resilient than Georgia was.

Robert's betrayal had wrecked her for a long time. But they'd also been married a long time. Maybe the heartache you felt was equal to the years you'd spent with your betrayer.

Georgia lifted her head and put those thoughts behind her. She just sat, listening to the waves and soaking in the peacefulness of it all. Once again, the intense feeling of being blessed came over her. Hard not to feel that way when this amazing view was hers to enjoy whenever she liked.

Clyde finished up his meal and came to sit by her. She reached down and gave his head a scratch. Robert had been dead set against pets of any kind. She scratched Clyde's head a little more and smiled.

A few minutes later, Mia walked back to the deck and sat in the other chair. She took a sip of her wine from the glass Georgia had brought out, then put the glass down and showed Georgia a photo on her phone. "This one? Or..." She swiped to the next one. "This one?"

"Let me see the first one again."

Mia swiped back.

Georgia shook her head. "They're both beautiful, but the first one shows a little more beach. I think I'd go with that one."

"Okay, cool." Mia tapped away, then announced, "Posted."

"That's for the new Sea Glass Inn account?"

"It is."

"How's it going?"

Mia shrugged. "I've only made a handful of posts. Hard to tell yet."

"You should put Clyde on there. He's going to be a permanent resident of the inn. And I'm not going to hide that fact, so you might as well include him. After all, aren't cats pretty popular on social media?"

"Very," Mia answered. She aimed her phone at him. "And I think that's a great idea. Not everyone will love it, though."

"I know," Georgia said. "I thought about that. Talked to Travis about it too. He said Aunt Norma made it plain that the inn was a cat-friendly establishment. At least friendly to Clyde. And if people didn't like it, then they just shouldn't come."

"Are you taking the same approach?" Mia started typing again, presumably to go with Clyde's picture.

Georgia shrugged. "Worked for Aunt Norma."

"You know," Mia said. "I've been doing a lot of thinking about opening this place and how to do it right and how to get us off to the best start."

"Me too. Although maybe not as much as you have. What are you thinking about?"

"Well, for starters, how do you feel about going through Aunt Norma's old registries and sending a personal note to all the regulars that the inn is back up and running? When it actually is back up and running, I mean. I know it's been a few years, but if they were regulars once, why wouldn't they want to come back again?"

Georgia's lips parted but for a moment, no sound came out. "That is brilliant. I don't know why I didn't think of it, but then I'm not surprised you did."

Mia grinned. "Thanks. The best part is we could actually get to work on that right away. As in we could start figuring out who to send those notes to, then start writing the notes. We just won't mail them until we're ready. But handwriting them would be a nice touch. And you have beautiful penmanship."

"That's perfect. Think about it, we could potentially reopen with a full house." Georgia shook her head. "Wouldn't that be amazing?"

"It would be. Of course, I don't even know what Aunt Norma charged. We need to figure out pricing, too. Although maybe we could charge a reduced rate for past guests? I don't know. We need to do the math on that."

Georgia nodded. "We have a lot to figure out. And weeks of work ahead of us. But this is excellent. You have any more ideas in that crafty head of yours?"

Mia's smile turned slightly secretive. "I do. But they're not formed enough for me to talk about. Right now, I'm focusing on the Instagram account. And getting the inn ready, obviously. But when the other ones are good enough to share, you'll be the first to know."

"I can't wait," Georgia said.

"I'm also planning on Instagramming the work on the inn and the progress as we go along. Unless you don't like that idea. I'm no Griffin when it comes to taking pictures, but I can get decent enough shots. I was thinking it might get people invested in the place. You know how popular DIY and fixer-upper shows are on TV. This could be sort of similar."

Georgia shook her head. "You're a genius. I love it." She lifted her glass. "Here's to my incredibly smart daughter."

Mia laughed and lifted her glass as well. "And here's to my incredibly wonderful mother for including me. And giving me a safe place to land when I needed it most."

"Always," Georgia said, her mind immediately going to Griffin. If only her son would let her know he was all right, everything would be perfect.

Maggie Miller

Chapter Twenty-one

Mia handed Mrs. Franklin her grocery receipt. "Thank you for shopping at Ludlows. Have a great day."

As Mrs. Franklin left, Lucas swung by. "How's it going?"

"Good. I feel like I totally have the hang of things. Maybe not the gift cards yet, but I'll get there."

"Yeah," he said. "Those can be tricky. Would you be able to pick up a shift next Friday? Susan needs a day off to chaperone her kid's field trip."

"Absolutely, I'd be happy to do it."

"Great, thanks. I'll make the change on the schedule."

There was no one in her line so she took the opportunity. "Can I ask you a question?"

"Sure."

"Does Ludlows ever sponsor events? Or co-sponsor them?"

His gaze narrowed in thought. "We've done some things like that. We've helped with food drives for the local food bank and one for a pet rescue." He leaned against her station. "Something in mind?"

"Maybe." She smiled. "But it's just a thought at the moment. An idea in progress, you might say."

"Is this about the inn?"

She laughed. "You're very perceptive."

He grinned. "Well, let me know when you want to talk more. We could even do it over lunch. If you want."

"I will. Thanks." She turned toward the customer who'd just entered her line. "Good morning."

As she rang them up, she let her mind wander to her idea and what might be possible if Ludlows got involved. It was shaping up, that much was clear.

Now she just had to make sure all her ducks were in a row and present the idea to her mother.

* * *

Carefully balanced on a step stool, Georgia wiped the sweat off her brow, then went back to trimming the crepe myrtle. The trees would be gorgeous when they bloomed. She wondered what color they were. Travis would probably know.

He was up on the roof, hammering away as he put the new shingles down. As soon as he called, she'd go over and hold the ladder for him so he could come down.

The man was an incredibly hard worker. Georgia was once again happy to have him on her team. Just one more thing to be thankful to Aunt Norma for.

She went back to work, trimming the tree. She had five more to go before she moved on to her next task. She wasn't sure what that was going to be yet.

The window boxes needed to be redone, but she wasn't sure if she should wait and do them closer to reopening or now. Whatever she put in them, she wanted them to be bright and colorful and overflowing. The kind of thing that always looked so pretty and welcoming in magazines.

Travis's hammering continued. She'd wanted to ask him if his daughter had called last night, but after their talk yesterday she thought maybe it was better to let him bring up the subject. She hadn't said anything about their talk to Mia either. Again, it was Travis's news to share, not hers.

Her mind went back to the window boxes. She really did need to know what color the crepe myrtles were. That would help her decide what to put in the window boxes. She wanted to make sure it all went together. She glanced over her shoulder at the front porch, giving it a quick assessment.

Maybe she should put herbs in some of those window boxes. Or maybe do a couple of big potted rosemary plants by the front door. Wasn't rosemary supposed to be a symbol of welcoming? Georgia couldn't remember, but it was worth looking up.

She thought about Mia's idea of Instagramming all the progress on the inn. The more Georgia thought about it, the more it seemed like a good idea. People did love fixer upper shows on television. Why wouldn't they want to see the same kind of thing on social media?

The next time she took a break, she texted Mia to encourage her to really go forward with Instagramming the progress on the inn. Although maybe Mia wasn't supposed to get personal messages at work. Then again, Georgia supposed if that were true her phone was probably tucked away somewhere.

Georgia went back to work trimming the tree and getting it into a good shape. Another few minutes went by and her phone rang. She laid her trimmers on the top of the step stool and got her phone out. It was Travis, ready to come down off the roof. She tilted her head and listened. Sure enough, the hammering had stopped. She smiled. Did that mean the roof was done? If so, they were that much closer to reopening.

She climbed off the step stool and went to hold the ladder. Travis was standing on the edge of the roof looking down.

"All done?" she asked.

"All done," he answered as he swung his leg around and got a foothold on the first rung. He started down.

"That's great."

"Well, we'll see after the next rain."

He was about half-way down, so she moved out of the way. "What's next?"

He touched down on solid earth. "Next, I'm going inside to have a closer look at the ceiling where the water damage was."

"I thought you checked that already."

"I did, but I brought my moisture meter today. If there's a sign of dampness, I'll probably cut out that section of drywall and replace. I may have to do more than that, depending on how things look behind there. If it's dry and solid, I'll just repaint it."

"Okay." But it concerned her that once again, a bigger repair bill could be on its way.

"How are the trees coming?"

"Slower than I'd hoped."

He smiled. "That's usually how all of this work goes." He adjusted his baseball cap. It was embroidered with the words *Taylor's Handyman Services*. "Speaking of work, I should have a look in the attic too. Make sure there's not any water damage in there. I meant to do that yesterday, but time got away from us."

Georgia frowned. "Wait. There's an attic?"

He nodded. "Didn't you and Mia check it out the other day? I thought you went through the whole place?"

"We did, but neither of us saw any attic entrance. Is it hidden like the office door?"

"Not really, but I suppose if you didn't know what it was, you might not realize it leads to an attic."

She glanced up at the house. "Now I'm curious as to what's in there."

"Come on, I'll show you the door."

Together they went inside and all the way upstairs to the beautiful suite.

He pointed at a door on the far side of the large landing that made up part of the suite's sitting room. "That's it right there."

"I thought that was a linen closet. I guess since it's right next to the bathroom."

"You want to come in with me for the inspection?"

"Sure, but I'm leaving the house side of things up to you."

He nodded. "No problem. But first..." He went over to the spot of discoloration on the ceiling and tapped it. "Sounds all right. That doesn't mean it is, though." He took a small device out of his toolbelt and turned it on, then held it against the spot.

"Is that the moisture meter?"

"It is." He stuck the device back in his toolbelt. "And it looks like we're good to repaint."

"Excellent news!" And a huge relief. She started for the attic door. "Now let's see if our good fortune lasts."

She tried the handle, but the door didn't open. "I think it's locked."

Travis put a hand on his head. "Yep, I'm sure it is. I forgot about that. She always kept it locked since it was off-limits to guests."

Georgia sighed. "I'll have to go back to the house. The lawyer gave me a huge bunch of keys. I'm sure the right one's on there."

"No need," Travis said. "She always kept one in her office. Unless that one is now on your keyring, but judging by the way her office looked yesterday, I think that space remained untouched. I'll go down and get it. No point in us both climbing all those stairs again."

"I don't mind getting it."

"But you won't know where to look."

"True." She smiled. "Okay, thanks."

"Be right back." He started down and she went to look out the windows at the beach.

Her phone dinged with an incoming text, reminding her that she needed to touch base with Mia anyway. She took her phone out and checked the screen.

Her heart leaped. The text was from Griffin in response to the picture she'd sent last night. It was short but it was still a response. Enough to let her know he was alive.

Looks great.

She quickly texted back, *You should see it for yourself.*

Not ten seconds later, he answered. *Maybe I will.*

Anytime, Georgia responded.

But nothing followed from Griff. She smiled anyway. Then she dashed off a longer text to Mia, letting her know to go full steam ahead with the Instagram account. And that Georgia had heard from Griffin.

Mia would probably want her to wait to explore the attic, but Travis needed to get in there, so it couldn't be put off. Because of that, Georgia left that bit out.

Travis returned, key in hand and not even breathing heavy from the stairs. That was impressive. He dangled the key off his finger. "Got it."

He went right for the door and unlocked it, then stepped inside and ran his hand over the wall for the light. Georgia couldn't see a thing inside. The attic had no windows. Finally, he found the switch and flipped it on.

"Wow," she said. "This is bigger than I expected. And what are all these boxes?"

"Some of it's Cecil's, I think," Travis said. "But most of it's hers. Lots of Christmas decorations, but also some personal stuff too."

Georgia made a beeline for a large, ivory box sealed in plastic wrap. Even without the clear window on the front of the box, she knew what it was.

A wedding dress.

Maggie Miller

Chapter Twenty-two

Georgia held the box toward the light. "I wonder if this is from her wedding to Cecil?" How amazing would it be to have that dress? They weren't a family big on tradition but that seemed like such a dear object to have that Georgia instantly felt sentimental.

Travis had a flashlight out and was shining at the roof, doing his inspection. "You could always find her wedding album and compare it."

"Not a bad idea. But then I'd have to unwrap the dress, and this looks so well-preserved I'd kind of hate to do that."

He looked over. "If that dress is really supposed to be preserved, I'm not sure this attic is the best place for it."

"Good point. It is stuffy in here. I imagine it gets pretty hot up here."

"Not too bad." He pointed to a vent with his flashlight. "There's a roof fan that helps take the worst of it out. Still, this isn't conditioned space."

"Then I'm taking this back downstairs. At least until I know for sure what dress it is."

"Right," he said. "Who knows? Might be from her first marriage. Or her second."

Laughing softly, Georgia nodded. "With Aunt Norma, it could be from any of them."

"You must have known the first two."

"Bartholomew Merriweather was the man I called uncle. Uncle Bart, to be exact. She loved him very much. Maybe not as much as Cecil, I'm not sure. But I remember that funeral even though I was pretty young."

"Yeah?" Travis asked as he inspected the back wall. "What was it like? Big?"

She put the box down by the door as she nodded. "It seemed big to me, but then I was just a kid. What I really remember is how beautiful Aunt Norma looked. She had on this immaculate black suit, black gloves, and a little black hat with a whisp of a veil that came down over her eyes. It was more like netting really. But I thought she looked like a movie star."

"That sounds very much like her."

"She never did anything in half measures, that's for sure." Georgia had a look around at what else there was in the attic. A dressmakers form. Some miscellaneous pieces of furniture. A standing coat rack. Plenty of boxes, all stacked neatly. Most of them seemed to be labeled, which was good.

She put her hands on her hips and took it all in. At some point, it would have to all be gone through. But that wasn't going to happen anytime soon. There was too much other work to be done. Maybe it was something she and Mia could tackle box by box as they got closer to the opening date. Then again, they might be too busy with preparing for that first guest.

She turned to look at Travis. "How's it going? Find anything I should know about?"

He shook his head. "Nothing yet. Which is good."

"I'll say. You mind if I go ahead and take this box downstairs? Or do you think you'll need me for something else?"

"Go on. I'm just about done. It all looks sound. I'll get that spot on the ceiling painted, then I'm going to start repairs on the porch balusters and railings. Got to make sure those are all sturdy."

"Okay. I suppose I should get back to my trees, too." She picked up the wedding dress box. "That reminds me. I need the number for the painters so they can come out and give me some estimates?"

"You mean the guy I know or the second company?"

She smiled. "Both of them."

"I'll give them to you when I get back outside."

"Thanks." She headed downstairs and back to Norma's bedroom, which she really needed to start thinking of as her own, but that was probably not going to happen until she was moved in.

Something else she needed to talk to Travis about. With the roof repaired and everything seeming to be in good order, there shouldn't be anything holding that up. Then she'd have to figure out the best way to rent the cottage. A real estate agent, she supposed.

She put the box on Norma's bed and took a look at the space. There wasn't all that much to be done, other than packing up Norma's things.

Georgia smiled. She'd probably end up putting some of them in the attic. She wasn't quite ready to get rid of all of them. It just felt too soon. And too impersonal. These things had meant something to Aunt Norma.

For that reason alone, it seemed like they ought to mean something to Georgia as well. She lingered a moment longer, then finally went back out to the crepe myrtles. There was too much work to do to stay inside and ponder the future.

She could ponder while she trimmed branches.

Something, that thankfully, Travis had known how to do. In fact, he wasn't only teaching Mia things, he was teaching Georgia some as well. Like how the blooms on crepe myrtle only came from new growth so if she wanted a tree full of flowers, it was best to prune it.

She climbed to the top rung of her step stool and took up her long trimming shears. Not that these trees wouldn't have gotten pruned anyway. They were a little wild and had lost their shape.

Fortunately, pruning them wasn't too hard the way Travis explained it.

She'd followed his instructions perfectly, starting with taking off all the low branches so that the trees' trunks would be nice and clean looking until the foliage started. She'd also removed the new shoots coming out of the ground. Suckers, he'd called them.

Then the most difficult bit happened. The cutting back of the tree while keeping a nice, rounded shape. It seemed to be going all right so far, though.

She kept snipping and trimming and cutting, until she heard the door behind her. With one hand on the step stool, she turned to look.

Travis was coming out of the house.

"How do they look so far? Okay?" she asked.

He peered at the trees for a long moment, then finally nodded. "Yep. Looks great. You're a natural. Maybe a little more off the top."

She frowned. "I can't reach that very well."

He came down the stairs toward her. "You need an actual ladder. That step stool isn't going to cut it. Fortunately, we have one. I'll get it." He hesitated. "You're not afraid of going up a little higher, are you?"

"No." She gave him a slightly stern look.

"Well, you can't blame me for asking. You were worried about me being on the roof."

"You were three floors up. We're just talking about another foot or two." She rolled her eyes. "I'm not a scaredy-cat. I was just concerned about you. Men are more accident-prone than women. Everyone knows that."

"Oh, right, that." There was a twinkle in his eye. "I'll just go get that ladder. I'll try not to hurt myself on the way there."

She would have put her hands on her hips if not for the trimmer in her grasp, but she was laughing on the inside. It was such a pleasure working with a guy like Travis. He was so easy going and laid back. Patient, too. Never seemed bothered by much. Always had a smile on his face.

Considering the situation with his daughter, he could have been a very different man. Or at least had a very different outlook on life.

Had Aunt Norma known about his grandson? She must have. That seemed like a thing he would have shared with her at some point in their years of friendship.

Travis came back with the tall folding ladder and set it up next to her step stool. "All right, give that a try."

She came down with her trimmers and climbed back up again on the new ladder. She got to the third rung and it wobbled.

Travis grabbed it. "Ground might be a little soft. I'll hold it."

Which meant he'd be looking right at her backside. "It's fine. You can go do your work."

"I wouldn't dream of it. And leave you here to fall? Nope. I'm going to stay right here and hold on to this just like you did for me."

She was thankful he couldn't see her face. Her cheeks felt hot so she had to be blushing. She closed her eyes and stepped up one more rung. She felt the kind of silly mortification that only a woman of her age could feel. But there was nothing she could do about it but get the job done and get off the ladder.

She started trimming away at the top branches with serious purpose.

"Hey," Travis said. "Take it easy. You're pruning them, not punishing them for growing."

She snuck a glance over her shoulder. He was looking up at her. She said a little prayer he couldn't see up her shorts. "I really don't need you to hold the ladder."

"Just finish the trimming."

With a sigh, she did just that. But in her mind, this made them even. She'd seen him in a towel and now he'd been up close and personal with her posterior. They were completely and totally square.

She finished the tree and looked at him again. "Why don't you step back and see what you think?"

"Okay."

As soon as he did, she got down. "Well?"

"Looks good to me." He was smiling. A lot.

She got the feeling he wasn't just talking about the tree.

He nodded at the ladder. "Why don't you do the tops of all of them while I'm here to hold the ladder, then you can do the rest with the step stool and I can get to work on the porch?"

She made a face before she could stop herself.

"What's wrong?" he asked.

"Nothing." She smiled to reassure him. "That's a great idea." What else could she say?

He picked up the ladder and moved it to the next tree.

"Hey, now that you've fixed the roof, when do you think Mia and I could move in?"

He had one hand on the ladder. "I'd say anytime you want. We still need to have the HVAC looked at but that shouldn't cause you any problems."

"That's great." She started up the ladder, happy to have a topic that would occupy them both. "We can get moved in right away. What real estate agent did Norma use to rent the cottage? I'll need to talk to them."

"No real estate agent. She used one of those vacation rental websites. Which reminds me, I called both painters. My buddy will be here tonight, and the other company will come by tomorrow to look the place over so they can do estimates. I also have the HVAC company Norma always used coming the day after tomorrow to tune up the system and see what kind of shape it's in."

She trimmed the treetop as quickly and neatly as she could. "Thank you, that was nice of you to make those calls."

"No worries," he said. "I had the time and I figured you were busy with this."

"I am, but I still could have done it. What's a vacation rental website?"

"You know, like VRBO or one of those."

She shook her head. "I'm not familiar with those. I'm sure Mia is, though."

"You might be able to just activate her old listing. Maybe. You'd probably have to find her account information and all that."

Georgia finished up the tree and came down. It looked very flat with just the top done. "Hey, you said Aunt Norma wasn't a big fan of computers. Now you're telling me she used a website to rent the cottage?"

He nodded as he moved the ladder to the next tree. "It was her one concession. And she hated to admit she used one, but I know for a fact she had a tablet. Not sure where that is now. Maybe in her nightstand? Or in a drawer in her office? Couldn't tell you. But she definitely had one."

"There must have been something pretty special about that website for her to forego the use of a real estate agent."

He snorted. "I think it had more to do with the fact that Lavinia Major, the main agent in town, was also the woman

Herb Sorenson took up with after he and Norma were done. Or maybe just before they were done. If you catch my drift."

"I do." Georgia propped her elbow on one of the ladder's rungs. "But who is Herb?"

Travis chuckled softly. "Have you heard about how your aunt got that third story?"

"Mr. Gillum mentioned she had a very special relationship with one of the town councilmen."

Travis nodded. "Herb Sorenson was that town councilman. And they were quite the item all throughout the building of Sea Glass House. He even cut the ribbon on the day the inn opened."

Georgia's mouth came open. "Go on."

"Well, apparently Norma found out that Herb and Lavinia had started up while she thought Herb was her one and only. Your aunt wasn't the kind to take that lying down, so she immediately wanted to cancel her rental contract on the cottage with Lavinia, which she couldn't do because a contract was a contract."

Georgia nodded. "Makes sense."

"But the contract gave your aunt the right to refuse any guest. Which she did. To every possible contract Lavinia brought her for the cottage. And just to really rub it into Lavinia's face, your aunt let people stay in the cottage rent free for the entire year that contract was valid. Soon as it expired, she took over the rentals herself until the website came along and then she moved it there."

"I'm surprised she didn't take Lavinia to court."

"There were …other circumstances." He shook his head. "Nothing that matters now. Anyway, after it was all said and

185

done, she refused to do business with another realtor ever again."

"That sounds like her. Cross her once and you'd never cross her again. Not if she could help it. Wow. Wait until I tell Mia."

"Speaking of, you'd better get to work on the rest of those trees or your daughter's going to wonder what you've been doing all day. She's liable to think we've been standing around talking."

It was Georgia's turn to laugh. "Well, it hasn't been all day." But she climbed up the ladder all the same.

Chapter Twenty-three

Mia had been thrilled to get her mom's text about going forward with documenting the inn's reopening on social media. So thrilled she started a Facebook page for the inn as soon as she got back to the cottage. She figured that was just one more potential audience, so why not? Especially when it wasn't that much more work.

But she was also very happy that her brother had finally been in touch. It bothered Mia that he hadn't responded to either of their efforts to contact him for so long. He'd always been a great brother and friend to her and having him drop out of her life just wasn't acceptable.

To be honest, she was also a little hurt to think he might be going through something that he wasn't sharing with her. But was that her fault? She knew they'd grown a little distant lately. She'd been occupied with the overwhelming task of wedding planning. The early stages when everything seemed like a good idea and it was all deliciously irresistible.

Thankfully, that was over.

But Griffin had also been focused on building his photography business. He'd been just as busy, if not more so, than she had been. So really the blame for their distance had to be shared equally.

Either way, Mia thought, that had to stop. They needed to reconnect and soon.

Because she was thinking about him, she pulled out her phone and sent her brother a quick text. Just a simple *hey how are you hope to talk to you soon.* Then she set her phone on the counter and went to change out of her Ludlows shirt and khaki pants, both of which she'd have to wash tonight.

Once she was in shorts and a T-shirt, she ate a quick PB&J, then grabbed her phone and headed to the inn to get to work. On her walk over she checked her messages. Nothing from Griff. Yet.

Travis was on the front porch working on the railings. Her mom was up on a tall step stool trimming the crepe myrtle trees that lined the front fence. Travis's back was to Mia, but she gave her mom a wave. "Hey Mom. How's it going?"

"Good, honey. How was work?"

"Pretty good."

"Walk back to the porch and tell me how the trees look. You kind of lose perspective being this close."

Mia did as her mom asked, catching Travis's eye as she approached.

He nodded at her. "Hey there."

"Hey." She looked at the trees to assess her mom's work. After a few moments, she pointed to the middle one on the left side. "That one needs more off the underneath section closest to you. Otherwise they look really nice."

Georgia gave her a thumbs up. "Thanks!"

Mia walked back over. "You guys sure have been busy."

Georgia came down off the ladder. "You have no idea. This place has an attic, which we went into so Travis could check for water damage in there. None, thankfully, but it's full of boxes and furniture and other stuff. I found a wedding dress. I'm pretty sure it's Aunt Norma's but I don't know what marriage it's from."

"Just the one dress?"

Georgia nodded. "I didn't see any others, but there's a lot up there. Could be another one."

"I bet it's from her wedding to Cecil." Mia grinned. "I forgot to tell you, but I found the top tier of her wedding cake perfectly preserved in the freezer when I was cleaning it out."

Georgia put a gloved hand to her heart. "That is so sweet. You saved it, right?"

"Absolutely. In fact, I'd love to find a way to preserve it permanently. After all, Cecil was the origin story for this inn."

"Origin story?" Her mother asked.

"You know, the real reason this inn exists. Aunt Norma built it because he bought her the lot and left her the money and it was going to be their dream house but they never had the chance. It feels to me like that should be a part of the inn going forward. In some way. Which I'm kind of working on an idea for."

"Oh? Tell me!"

Mia shook her head. "It's still forming but as soon as it feels solid, I'll share it. But that wedding dress is equally inspiring. What did you do with the dress?"

"It's on the bed in Norma's room. The box is sealed so I didn't want to open it, but we should try to figure out if it's from her wedding to Cecil for sure."

"We can do that, I'm sure. Anything else new?"

"Yes," Georgia said brightly. "Travis says the house is sound enough for us to move into. Isn't that great? We can get the cottage rented sooner than I thought. Of course, we'll have to live here while there's work being done, but that shouldn't be too much of an inconvenience."

"Nah," Mia said. "We'll deal with it. A little pain for a lot of gain."

"Right," her mom said. "Which also reminds me that in the next few days we'll have an estimate for the painting *and* the HVAC guys are coming out to make sure that system is in good working order."

"Fantastic. Things are really moving along. Is there anything specific you need me to work on today?"

"As a matter of fact there is. Travis said Aunt Norma used a website to rent the cottage. Some kind of vacation rental home site? Do you know anything about that?"

"Sure," Mia said. "And I think that's a great idea. But I thought Aunt Norma didn't like computers?"

"Well, she liked real estate agents less, which is a story I'll tell you tonight while we're sitting on the back deck."

"I can't wait to hear it."

Her mom nodded, smiling. "You'll enjoy it, I'm sure. Anyway, Travis said there should be a tablet in either Aunt Norma's office or in her bedroom, maybe in the nightstand." Georgia glanced toward the house. "Do you think you can look for that? And do you think you can dig around in her office to see if you can find her password? That way we could just reactivate her account and get the cottage up for rent pretty quickly."

"Are you sure we shouldn't start a new account for ourselves?"

Georgia pursed her lips. "Won't that be a lot of work?"

Mia laughed softly. "Mom, the computer stuff is what I'm especially good at. It won't be work. I promise. At least it won't be work I mind doing. Then we won't have to worry about reconnecting the account. Although I'll still look."

"Okay, then that's your task for today. You could also take a peek at that second bedroom and see what needs to be done so that you can move in."

"What about your room? Aunt Norma's?"

Georgia sighed. "Is it weird that I feel odd about moving her stuff out of there?"

"No, I get it. It's like removing her from her home, right?"

Her mom nodded. "Yeah, it's just like that."

"What would Norma want you to do?"

Georgia's expression changed instantly. "Toss her stuff out and move in."

Mia snorted. "Well, we're not tossing her stuff out. But I could certainly work on clearing out that space. Maybe boxing some things up? Or do you want to do that?"

"If it's all just going to go in the attic, I think you could do it. But don't throw anything out unless you show it to me first."

"I wouldn't dream of it. And the sooner those rooms are ready, the sooner the cottage can go up for rent, right?"

"Right."

Mia turned toward the house. "Then I'm on it." She took a step, then stopped and looked at her mom again. "Did you guys eat lunch yet?"

"Yes. We had sandwiches. At our own homes. Why?"

Mia shrugged. "Just making sure you're not overworking yourselves, that's all. I had a sandwich too. PB&J. Now I'm ready to make some progress inside. If I find anything good, I'll call you."

"Okay, thanks." Smiling, Georgia climbed back up the ladder, grabbed her trimmers and went back to work.

Mia went into the house, bypassing Travis who was meticulously measuring a piece of wood. Inside, it was cooler and quieter, but still looked very much like a house on hold. All of the furniture was still covered over with drop cloths. She couldn't wait until those were gone, but she wasn't sure she should take them off just yet.

If the floors had to be redone and everything dusted, that was only going to kick up more grime. Didn't make sense to uncover what would only have to be recovered.

She went straight back to Aunt Norma's room. A large ivory box sat on the bed, the wedding dress her mother had mentioned. Mia walked over and put her hands on the sides of it. She could see hints of the gown through the clear window on the front of the box. Mostly it looked like satin, Italian satin maybe. There were a few small fabric roses as well, made out of the same satin, and a dusting of clear sequins.

The dress looked remarkably restrained, which wasn't how Mia would have pictured Aunt Norma's dress. Her limited memories of Norma were much more over the top. But she liked that whatever lay preserved in this box was definitely a statement of who her aunt had been at that time. And how happy she'd been about the man she was marrying.

Mia had looked at a lot of wedding dresses lately. Well, not lately. Not since she found out about Brendan's cheating. But in the days before that she'd looked through more bridal magazines than she could count, dog-earing the pages with the dresses she liked best.

She knew her mom hadn't opened the box because it was so well sealed, but Mia was dying to see the dress inside. Aunt Norma's taste seemed to run towards the unusual and the interesting, and Mia had no doubt that the wedding dress, even if it was restrained, would be something that fit that description.

The solution was to find Aunt Norma's wedding photos. There had to be some. Mia couldn't imagine she'd married Cecil and not documented it with at least one picture.

But Mia also had to find her aunt's tablet. And password. Not that she thought either one was necessary, but it was worth a look if she was going to dig around for a wedding photo as well.

She started with the top drawer of the nightstand on the right-hand side and found the tablet immediately. She laughed. "That was easy."

Of course, the tablet was dead. Thankfully, there was a charger cable in the drawer as well. She got that plugged in and charging, then went back to her search. The rest of the nightstand drawer held bits and pieces of Norma's life.

A sleep mask, a bottle of moisturizer, a nail file, a pack of tissues, two kinds of lip balm, a notebook and several pens, a romance novel…all the usual suspects.

No photos, though. Odd there wasn't a picture of Cecil nearby. Could she have taken it to the nursing home with her?

That seemed like a possibility. But anything she'd taken should have been returned.

Mia kept digging, doing a cursory search of the other nightstand, which was almost empty, and her aunt's dresser. Nothing but clothes in the drawers, except for the top drawer which had been fitted with a velvet lining and held the most amazing display of costume jewelry Mia had ever seen.

She wasn't much of a jewelry person, especially not extravagant pieces, but there was something so captivating about her aunt's collection. Big, beaded necklaces in bright colors, some with tassels, some with pendants like an enormous talon (probably not real, Mia imagined) or a carved parrot on a swing. Equally bright earrings and bracelets and rings, too.

There was no shortage of bling in the drawer either. Plenty of rhinestones and crystals and glittery bits.

Mia just shook her head in admiration. "I wish I could have known you better."

It was easy to see why her mom missed this remarkable woman so much. Every time Mia learned something new about her aunt, she liked her that much more.

Finally Mia went to the closet. She'd opened it briefly the last time she'd been in this room but hadn't really paid attention to what was in it. This time, she did.

She opened the closet and had a closer look. Lots of sundresses front and center so that had to be what her aunt had worn the most. Some pretty blouses toward the front, too, along with some light cardigans and a few summer-weight sweaters.

But toward the back, things got more interesting. There were a few evening things. Cocktail dresses. A sequined jacket. Satin pants and a flowing, iridescent silk blouse. Behind those, were several outfits in garment bags.

Mia took the first one out, laid it on the bed and unzipped it. A suit of gorgeous nubby fabric, primarily ivory but with flecks of other colors woven in. Something about it seemed familiar. Maybe it was just the classic shape.

She caught sight of the distinct gold signature buttons and her mouth came open in surprise. Could it really be?

She pushed the garment bag out of the way a little more and opened the jacket up. A thin line of delicate chain trimmed the inside hem where the fabric met the silk lining. And the label said Chanel.

Maggie Miller

Chapter Twenty-four

"Mom. Mom. *Mom.*"

Georgia turned to see Mia running out of the house. Fearing the worst, she quickly got down off the ladder. "What's wrong?"

"Nothing's wrong. I was about to start packing up Aunt Norma's room and I just found a Chanel suit in her closet. A Chanel *suit*. And when I looked through her closet I found a bunch of other designer stuff. Handbags and shoes and more clothes. Some of her jewelry is designer, too. And there's a couple pieces I wasn't sure about but I'm going to research them and see what I can figure out."

"Well, that's all very interesting." Georgia wasn't sure what to do with the information her daughter had just given her.

"Mom, don't you see? That stuff is worth money."

Georgia appreciated Mia's enthusiasm, so she chose her words carefully. "Honey, it's old, though. And used."

Mia shook her head. "You're adorable. I'm totally keeping you. Never change, Georgia Carpenter, never change."

Georgia crossed her arms. "Okay, smarty pants, what's the big deal with the clothes? Are they really worth that much?"

Mia nodded, clearly excited by her finds. "Yeah, they are." She pulled out her phone and started tapping away. "Hang on, I'll show you."

A couple seconds later, Mia turned her phone around. "This is a popular resale site. Look at that suit. It's almost identical to the one I found in Aunt Norma's closet."

Georgia shielded the screen with her hand to see it better. "Mm-hmm. Very nice."

"Look at the price."

Georgia located it. And looked closer. She stared for a second longer. "That can't be right. Twelve hundred dollars?"

With a triumphant nod, Mia took her phone back. "For a classic Chanel suit with the logo buttons? You betcha."

"Wow. I had no idea." Georgia's gaze shifted to the house. "Aunt Norma is a gift that keeps on giving." She looked at her daughter again. "Are you proposing taking on the job of selling that stuff?"

Mia nodded. "Why not? I mean, those things should go to someone who will use them right?" She smiled. "And who's willing to pay for them."

Georgia laughed. "I second that."

"Although…I don't think it would be so terrible if you want to keep some of it."

Georgia thought about that a moment. "I don't know. Might be better to have the money with all that needs to be done."

Mia shrugged. "Your call. But I still want you to look at all of it before any of it goes up for sale."

"I will."

"You will what?" Travis asked. He'd come along with some scraps for the trash.

"Mia found some potentially valuable designer things in Norma's wardrobe. She wants me to look at them before she sells them."

Travis nodded. "She talked about some of that stuff. I think a lot of it was from her honeymoon wardrobe. That cruise around the world they took was pretty fancy. Cecil bought her a...I can't remember what she called it. An old-fashioned word that means wedding wardrobe, I think."

"Trousseau?" Georgia offered.

"Yeah, that's it. Cecil bought her a trousseau of all kinds of high-end clothes and shoes and handbags. Jewelry, too, I think. She loved telling that story and talking about how she was the best dressed woman on the cruise."

Georgia pondered that. "Did she wear any of that stuff after the cruise? In her life as an innkeeper, I mean?"

Mia's brows went up as though she couldn't wait to hear the answer.

Travis nodded. "She did, actually. I know because any time she had a piece of it on, she'd tell me it was from that collection. She had a white suit she used to wear a lot." He laughed suddenly. "That was the suit she wore to the town council meeting where she was granted her third floor as a matter of fact."

"See, Mom?" Mia said. "Good stuff lasts a long time."

"I see," Georgia answered. "Maybe I *should* have a look at some of those things." Her wardrobe was pretty slim thanks to the divorce. "Although I'm not sure I'll have much use for anything too fancy."

"Well," Travis said. "There's always the inn's Christmas party. Should you decide to start it up again."

"Oh?" Georgia said. "Is that a tradition?"

"It was," he answered. "Once upon a time. A very popular tradition. Seemed like the entire town would turn out for that. And you better believe your aunt dressed up. So did most everyone else who attended. I'm pretty sure it was considered the social event of the season. It sort of kicked off the holiday celebrations in town."

Mia clapped her hands. "We have to bring that back. We have to."

Travis continued on to the trash bin at the curb. "It would be nice."

Georgia shook her head. "I don't know. Depends a lot on how the inn's doing, I suppose. Sounds expensive. But I'll think about it, how's that?"

"Think hard," Mia said, smiling. "Because if we reopen in December, the party would be the perfect way to celebrate that."

Georgia chuckled. "I will think about it. Promise. Now I'm getting back to work."

Mia held her hands up. "Me too!"

As Mia went back inside, Georgia climbed up the ladder to finish trimming the trees. She couldn't stop thinking about the Christmas party, though. It would be a fun thing to do. And a wonderful way to become part of the community while letting everyone know they were open for business again.

The real question was how much would a thing like that cost? And would they be able to afford it by then? It really depended on how much money it took to bring the inn back to life.

She spent the remainder of the afternoon finishing up the trees, gathering up the trimmed bits for disposal, and thinking about how amazing the inn would look decorated for Christmas. She almost laughed at herself.

Christmas was months away and yet she was already making plans.

Just as she was finishing up and preparing to weed the flower beds, a work truck parked alongside the curb. Travis stopped what he was doing, which was replacing one of the stair treads leading up to the porch and came to greet the man who got out of the truck.

"Georgia, this is Diego Santos. My buddy the painter I was telling you about."

Diego smiled and stuck his hand out. "Nice to meet you, ma'am."

She shook his hand. "Nice to meet you too. I hope you brought a sharp pencil with you today."

He laughed. "I promise to give you the best price I can." He looked at the house. "Do you want to change this color or keep everything the same?"

She didn't have to think about that. "Keep everything the same."

"All right. Let me get to work." He hesitated. "Do you want an estimate for the inside, too?"

Georgia thought for a moment, remembering her conversation with Mia about making Aunt Norma's room her own. "Actually, for a couple of the rooms, yes. Would you like me to show you which ones they are now or after you're done with the outside?"

"You can show me now."

"Okay, let's go in." She took her gloves off and laid them over one of the rungs of the ladder, then led him inside.

The cool air was nice. She looked at the walls with fresh eyes, trying to determine if a coat of paint was necessary anywhere else. Sure, they'd need some touching up, but they looked pretty good otherwise.

She went farther into the house. "Mia?" she called out.

"Back here, Mom."

"I have the painter with me."

Mia popped out of Aunt Norma's bedroom as they approached. "Are you getting the inside painted too?"

"I was thinking about doing our bedrooms and maybe the kitchen." She glanced at Diego. "Depending on the price."

He nodded. "Of course."

She showed him Aunt Norma's room. It was a soft, buttery yellow that was pretty, but a new color would definitely help Georgia think of the space as her own. "This is the first room. Then the kitchen out there, then there's another bedroom on the other side."

"Okay. I'll do some measurements."

Georgia left him to his work. She found Mia in the pantry, wiping down the shelves. "How's it going?"

"Good. I think it's a good idea, by the way."

"Repainting?"

She nodded. "Then it'll be more your room."

"That's what I was thinking." Georgia looked at her daughter. "I was going to have him price out the kitchen and your room, too."

Mia glanced toward the bedroom she'd soon be occupying. "I can live with that minty color."

Georgia's brows rose. "Mia. I happen to know you hate that color."

Mia shrugged. "Yeah, but it's money."

"And this is going to be our home. For a long, long time, I hope."

Diego called out to her. "Ms. Carpenter? Which room next?"

Georgia stuck her head out so she could see him through the breakfast room. "The kitchen." Georgia pointed toward what would be Mia's room. "And then the other bedroom on this side."

Mia smiled. "Thanks, Mom."

Georgia grinned. "Well, you're going to make all that money selling Aunt Norma's designer stuff, so why not?"

"Hey," Mia said. "Since you're inside, you should have a look at some of it. Especially this one purse I found. I think you should keep it."

"Okay, I'm game for a look." She went with Mia in the bedroom.

Mia opened up the closet and brought out a navy-blue tote bag with very familiar quilting and gold chain handle with leather threaded through it.

Even Georgia could identify that bag as Chanel. She nodded. "That is very pretty. And you know, Aunt Norma loved a tote bag like that. I remember as a child thinking her handbag held one of everything in the world."

Mia laughed. "This bag has room for a lot but I'm not sure it could hold that much. There are still a few things in it."

"Let me see." Georgia took the purse and sat down on the bed with it. In the side pocket was a lace-edge handkerchief, an old lipstick in the most vivid shade of pink, and half a ticket stub for a movie. She took it all out and set it on the bed. "Hang on, there's something else in there."

She took out the last thing. A small key with some pretty scrollwork on the top. A black ribbon was looped through the hole at the top and tied off.

"What do you think that's for?" Mia asked.

"No idea, but we probably shouldn't throw it away."

Mia nodded. "There's a couple hooks here in the closet you could hang it on. Are you going to keep that bag?"

It was lovely. And nicer than anything Georgia owned. "I don't know. Couldn't you get a lot of money for it?"

Mia nodded, a little reluctantly. "Probably but that doesn't mean I couldn't sell it at a later time."

"True." Georgia smoothed her hand over the amazingly soft leather. "You know, maybe we should hold on to most of these things. Like you said, we can always sell them later, right?"

"Right, we can." Mia had a hint of a smile on her face. "Feeling sentimental?"

"I am. A bit. But also just like we should wait. I don't know why. Just a feeling. It's not like I need that much closet space anyway."

"I'm cool with keeping them."

Diego called to them from the kitchen. "I'm all done. Going out to estimate the exterior."

"Thank you," Georgia answered.

Mia started for the door. "I should get back to work too. Although tomorrow I can work all day since I'm not scheduled at Ludlows. I'm going to run over there in the morning, though, so I can grab some empty boxes. Then my focus will be packing away anything we don't want in these two rooms."

"Great. Then as soon as they're painted, we can move in."

"And rent the cottage," Mia said. "Which reminds me, I found Aunt Norma's tablet but not her password. If you need me, I'll either be in her office having a look for that or finishing up in the pantry."

"Okay. Thanks, honey."

"Sure thing." Mia left.

Georgia stayed seated, the tote bag in her lap. She picked up the key and turned it over in her fingers, wondering what it might be for. Probably nothing, she thought.

Then again, with Aunt Norma, she could never be too sure.

Maggie Miller

Chapter Twenty-five

In a few more hours, Mia had finished the pantry and done a pretty thorough search of Aunt Norma's office. Unfortunately, she hadn't turned up anything resembling a password or a book she might have written it in. Didn't really matter. She thought it was better to set up a brand-new account on the HomeAway site anyway.

Of course, that meant she'd have to take brand new pictures, which she didn't love. Taking cute snaps for the Instagram account was one thing. Taking beautiful pictures meant to entice potential guests into renting the cottage was another.

In a moment of frustration, she sent a text to her brother. *I wish you were here.* She tossed the phone aside and went back to work with no expectations of an answer.

That work was Norma's closet. She sorted through everything, separating out the things worth keeping for resale and the stuff that could probably be donated. Even though the closet wasn't that full, it was a big job.

Possibly made bigger because each item had to be inspected. If something wasn't in good repair, Mia didn't want to donate it. Not surprisingly, Aunt Norma's things were all in excellent shape.

The keepers stayed in the closet. The donation pile accumulated on the bed and the floor, and that section probably made up three quarters of what had been in the closet.

Mia suspected the clothing in the dresser would be much the same. She was determined to get it all done, though. Tomorrow she wanted to box things up and make a run to Bon Voyage Vintage, the thrift shop near Ludlows.

In fact, she wondered if she could get the first batch done in the morning when she went to the store for boxes. Surely the thrift shop wouldn't mind if some things came in garbage bags, would they?

She made a quick phone call to confirm their hours and see if there were any criteria for dropping items off.

"Oh no," the woman said on the other end of the line. "We're happy to have anything. As long as the things are in reasonable shape, of course."

"Great," Mia said. "My aunt's stuff is in really good shape, I just have to finish sorting it."

"Do you need help? We do sometimes assist with estate sales, and things of that nature."

"No, I'm pretty close to being done. I'll bring over the first batch in the morning. I have to go to Ludlows and pick up boxes."

"Thank you for thinking of us."

"Sure," Mia said. "See you in the morning." She hung up. Wasn't like there was another thrift shop in town. Not that she knew about anyway.

She went to the pantry, found a couple kitchen trash sized garbage bags and started on the dresser. The clothing in it was a lot more casual. T-shirts and capri pants, things like that. Suddenly, Mia straightened and looked from the contents of the drawer in front of her to the things piled on the bed.

Not a single pair of jeans.

Could that be right? Did Aunt Norma not wear jeans? Mia smiled. She'd have to ask her mom about that.

Sorting the dresser went much faster than the closet. As Mia was lifting the last pile of things to put on the bed, she heard her mother's voice behind her.

"Are you still at it?"

Mia put the clothing down and turned. "Almost done."

"Wow, I can't believe you did all this." Georgia laughed. "You really knocked it out."

"Still more to go." Mia glanced at the closet. "I just realized I haven't gone through the shoes yet."

"You can do that in the morning."

Mia shrugged. "If you don't mind, I'd rather get it done now. I want to load some things into my car tonight too, that way when I go to Ludlows in the morning for boxes, I can drop off some of this at the thrift shop. I already told them I was coming, actually."

"It's up to you. But I'm about done."

Mia snorted. "You look done. You have dirt on your face and a leaf in your hair."

"Wouldn't surprise me." Georgia ran her hands through her hair, dislodging the stray bit of greenery. "There's pretty much nothing I want more right now than a hot shower and a glass of wine."

"You sure earned it. I'll finish up and then join you for a glass of that wine. Maybe another hour? Maybe not even that long."

"Okay." Georgia smiled. "Thank you for all your hard work."

"You're the one doing the hard work. You and Travis. I'm just sorting stuff."

Still smiling, her mom shook her head. "This is hard work too. Maybe not as sweaty and dirty, but equally important. See you at the cottage."

"Yep."

"Love you."

"Love you too."

Her mom left and Mia went back to the closet to sort the shoes. Most of them were in pretty good condition, but it was easy to see which ones had been Aunt Norma's favorites. There was a pair of well-worn espadrilles and another pair of slightly grungy sneakers. Although Mia couldn't imagine what outfits those sneakers had been worn with. Especially since her aunt had apparently not owned any jeans. Maybe some of the capri pants? Or the shorts?

And maybe those sneakers had been used for gardening? Mia wasn't sure, but they were going in the discard pile. Besides those two pairs of shoes, there were a lot of sandals and a good number of fancy high heels.

Again, the designer brands were interspersed with the ordinary ones. But all of them had a lot of flair. Bright colors, rhinestones, crystals, embellishments. There were patterned shoes too, florals and polka dots and even a pair of plaid ballet flats.

Mia shook her head. "Aunt Norma, you sure had style."

She quickly sorted through them. Designer shoes on the bed. And the rest that were in good condition were set aside to go to the thrift shop.

Mia got one of the kitchen-sized garbage bags out and started carefully filling it with clothes to be donated. When that bag was full, she moved on to the next one. She didn't like putting the things in garbage bags but without boxes she had no other choice. Before long she had four garbage bags filled with clothes and shoes. That would make for a nice drop off in the morning at Bon Voyage Vintage.

She thought about going to get her car and loading it up so it would be ready for the morning, but the weariness of the day had settled over her. All she really wanted to do was go back to the cottage and join her mom for that glass of wine. She turned off all the lights and headed for the door. She turned the lock and shut it, making sure it was secure. Then on a whim, instead of taking the sidewalk, she headed around the Inn to the back and the beach.

She stood on the deck looking towards the water. It was truly beautiful. And even though it wasn't sunset, she took out her phone to snap a couple pics.

A text message awaited her. She sucked in a breath. It was from Griff. Just a single emoji in response to her earlier text saying she wished he was here. The smiley face with his hand on his chin. The thinking emoji.

The message was a little cryptic, but also gave Mia hope that her brother could be thinking about visiting. Of course, with Griff, he might also mean he was trying to figure out what Mia and his mother were doing in Blackbird Beach.

For a split-second, she thought about calling him, but she had a feeling it would just go to voicemail. For whatever reason, Griff was keeping his distance from them.

She sighed and brought up her camera as she headed down to the water. The sky was golden with the sinking sun and the water gleamed like it had been gilded.

She took a few pictures then tucked her phone away. She'd look at them later and decide which one was gram worthy. But for now, she just wanted to enjoy this gorgeous place.

If she'd had the energy, she would have pulled off her socks and sneakers and dug her toes into the sand, but the day had gotten the best of her. She walked toward the cottage, watching the waterline for any interesting shells.

The walk back was short, but she'd found two shells and one small piece of white frosted beach glass she wanted to keep.

She held them in her hand as she went up to the back deck. Her mom was there, in one of the Adirondack chairs. Clyde sprawled between the two chairs, but he got up when he saw her, meowing as if to say, "Hurry up."

Georgia laughed. "He sure does like you."

Mia stepped onto the deck and reached down to scratch his head. "The feeling is mutual, isn't it, Clyde?"

He pushed against her hand.

She looked at her mom. "I'm going to take a quick shower and then I'll be out here with you."

Georgia nodded. "Sounds good."

Mia went in and put her findings from the beach in a little pile on the nightstand. She needed a jar to keep them in.

Maybe there was something at the inn she could use. Or maybe she could find something at the thrift shop.

She showered, put on fresh clothes, then grabbed a glass of wine and joined her mom and Clyde on the back deck, flipping on the hanging lights before she went out. The soft glow was so pretty. "What's for dinner?"

"Um...sandwiches?" Her mom laughed. "Today has left me a little brain dead."

"We still have leftover spaghetti," Mia said. Her poor mom. She looked tired. Not in such a bad way, but the day had definitely worn her out. "I could heat that up."

"That would be great. Thank you."

Mia set her wine down and got up to go do that, but she paused at the door. "I heard from Griff. Just a single emoji so not really anything to get excited about, but he must be okay. Or at least okay enough to text."

Her mom nodded. "That's good. I mean, it's something, right?"

"Right." But as Mia went inside to put the leftovers in the microwave, she couldn't help but wish it was a little something more.

She got the spaghetti out, popped it in to heat, then leaned on the counter and took out her phone. Maybe it was the long day getting to her, but she was suddenly tired of her brother's behavior. At least toward their mom. Brushing her off wasn't cool.

She shot off a text to him. *You need to talk to mom. She's worried about you. An emoji doesn't cut it. Call her.*

She hit send, instantly wondering if her text would just push her brother farther away or snap him out of whatever funk he was in.

Time would tell, she supposed. She glanced toward the deck. Meanwhile, their mother was the one bearing the weight of the worry. She already had a lot on her plate with working on the inn, she didn't need another burden.

Mia stirred the spaghetti, then put it back in for another minute, sighing as she pushed the buttons. "Do the right thing, Griffin. For all of us."

Chapter Twenty-six

After dinner, Georgia found enough energy to take a walk on the beach. She didn't have plans to go far, but her mind was restless with thoughts of Griffin and how much there was to do at the inn. She wouldn't sleep well if she couldn't sort some of that out. The sound of the waves was calming. Plus, she was discovering that a beach walk was a good way to think.

Besides, it was a walk not a jog. She'd go however far she felt like and then turn around and hopefully fall into bed, ready to sleep.

The moonlight was surprisingly adequate to light her path, but a few yards down the shore and she saw a small lantern on the beach. Someone was sitting on the sand about halfway between the water and the grassy dunes.

A little farther and she recognized the person. "Hey, Travis."

He nodded at her. "Georgia. I'm amazed you have the energy to walk."

She stopped a couple feet away. He had a camping lantern at his side. "I don't really, but it's helping me think."

"About the inn?"

She nodded. And her son, but that was a much more complicated answer.

He patted the sand. "You're welcome to join me."

That wasn't something she needed to think about. She walked over and took a seat. "How's your night?"

He was quiet for a long moment, then sighed. "Still no phone call."

"Sorry." She felt for him more than ever. "I've been trying to get a hold of my son, Griffin, and not having much luck either. I'm starting to wonder if my soon-to-be ex has turned him against me."

Travis shook his head. "Kids can break your heart, huh?"

"Yep."

"You're lucky you have Mia," he continued. "She's a great kid. Young woman, I should say. Smart, willing to learn, a real go-getter."

"Thanks. Wasn't always like that." Georgia smiled at the memory. "She was a handful as a teenager, but then I suppose they all are at that age."

"Sam was too. Before things got…complicated. She was a cheerleader and headstrong like her mother. A little spoiled, too. My fault, I'm sure, but it's hard not to spoil them when you love them so much."

"It is." Georgia hesitated a moment before asking the next question. "Have you tried calling her?"

"I used to. But she'd never answer. It would just go to voicemail. After a while, I stopped."

"What if…you sent her a picture of the inn and invited her to come for a visit with Clayton?"

"I don't know. Maybe." He stared out at the water. "It's hard to say what she'd do, although I'm guessing she'd ignore it, like everything else I've tried." He glanced down at the sand. "Man, I'd love to see that kid. Both of them. But missing out on Clayton's life is…"

She wasn't sure if emotion had cut him off, but she nodded when he went silent. "I know. I get it. I mean, I don't have any grandchildren, but I have a pretty good idea about what you're feeling."

"Thanks."

They sat in silence for a few moments, listening to the waves and looking at the stars. Then Travis took a deep breath and yawned. "I should go to bed. The other painting contractor will be here in the morning. And I have to fix that one window on the second floor. Plus the shower in the blue bathroom up there needs to be regrouted and two of the other bathrooms need new shower heads put on."

"I'm worn out just hearing about all that. But you're right, it's time for bed."

He smiled and got to his feet, picking up the lantern but holding his other hand out to her. She took it and let him help her up. He held her hand a second longer after she stood, finally letting it go when he asked, "When are you guys moving over to the inn?"

"After the interior painting is done." She could still feel the warm of his hand on hers.

"You know, not to undercut Diego, but if you want me to handle that, I can. Interior painting is no big deal."

"Oh. I hadn't thought about that. Okay, let me see how much extra it is."

"Besides the money, it would let him get started on the outside sooner."

"Something else I hadn't thought about. That's motivation enough. When could you do it?"

"As soon as I get the paint, pretty much."

She gave him a nod. "Deal. See you in the morning then. Maybe we can run to the hardware store and grab the paint, too."

"Sounds good." He held her eye contact. "Sleep well, Georgia."

"You too, Travis." Another moment passed between them, then she turned and walked back to the cottage, smiling.

Once again, she was reminded of how different Travis was from Robert. One of the biggest differences was that Travis had a heart. It was plain to see how much he loved and cared for his daughter and his grandson, even though he hadn't seen them in so very long.

Georgia hoped that that changed for him very soon. Just like she hoped that her situation with Griffin changed as well. Travis was right. Kids could break your heart.

When she got back to the cottage, she wiped her feet on the mat and went inside, locking the slider behind her and turning off the outdoor lights.

Mia was sitting on the sofa, watching television. Clyde was curled up next to her. He looked very happy. And very much asleep.

"I'm going to bed. See you in the morning, kiddo."

"Okay, mom." Mia grabbed the remote and turned off the television. "I should go to bed too. I wasn't really paying attention anyway."

"Don't do it on my account," Georgia said. "Stay up if you want to."

Mia picked Clyde up. "No, it's okay. Clyde's obviously ready to go in."

Georgia laughed. "I don't think he misses an opportunity to sleep. He'd be ready anytime."

Mia nodded. "No doubt that's true." She kissed the top of his head. "Good thing I set up a litter box in my bathroom, huh, you silly boy?"

He headbutted her.

She snorted. "I think that's a yes. See you in the morning. Love you, Mom."

"Night, honey. Love you too. Night, Clyde." Georgia went into her bedroom and checked her phone, just to see if there was any message from Griffin. There wasn't. Again. She sighed and put on her nightgown.

Maybe it was the long day, maybe it was the walk on the beach, but she fell asleep fast. When she woke up, light was just trickling in through the window and if she listened closely, she could hear the sound of the waves.

No, wait. That was rain.

"Ugh." She sat up. That wasn't going to help progress on any outside work. She pulled on her robe and went out to get coffee. Good thing there was so much to do inside.

Mia was already up. And dressed. And had coffee made. Also a plate with two pieces of peanut butter toast drizzled with honey sat at her spot at the table.

"Wow, you've been busy. When did you become an early bird?"

"When I had so much to do." Mia looked out the kitchen window. "I knew I should have packed my car last night. Now I have to do it in the rain."

"I'll help you. Then Travis and I can go to the hardware store." Georgia got a cup and filled it with coffee. "That reminds me. What color do you want your room?"

"Um…maybe just a soft sand color? Not beige exactly. But the color of the sand. You know what I mean?"

"I do." Georgia leaned against the counter and took a sip, letting the coffee bring her to life. "I was thinking about the same color myself. In fact, that will make it easier if we both do the same one."

"I'm good with whatever you pick out."

"For the kitchen, I was thinking butter yellow. Like a shade or two lighter than what Aunt Norma's room is now. What do you think?"

"I like that. What are you going to do about that awful linoleum?"

"I was trying not to spend the money, but it is bad, isn't it?"

Mia nodded. "And new paint is only going to make it look worse."

Georgia had a little more coffee. "I'll talk to Travis about that today. Maybe we should just put new linoleum down. It's long lasting and cheap."

Mia made a face. "I guess. Talk to Travis first, though, will you?"

"I promise. Now I'm going to get ready."

"I'm heading over as soon as I finish my breakfast. I'll see you there."

"Okay." Georgia started for the bathroom. A hot shower was calling her name. She stopped. "Where's Clyde?"

"Sleeping on my bed. He already ate. And has no interest in going out."

"I don't blame him." Georgia took her coffee with her.

She cranked on the water to let it warm up, then grabbed some clothes for the day. Jeans, a T-shirt and sneakers. Just right for working inside on a damp, rainy day. There was even a coolness to the air and for a moment, she wondered if she should take a sweatshirt, too.

While she was trying to decide, her phone rang. She checked the screen. Unknown number. Her mind went straight to Griffin. Excited, she answered it. "Hello?"

"Hello, Georgia."

A shiver of revulsion went through her at the sound of her husband's voice. "What do you want?"

"I'll cut right to it," he said. "I understand you've come into an inheritance."

Her jaw fell open. How did he know about the inn? She wanted to hang up on him, but she also wanted to know how he'd found that out. "I don't know what you mean."

He laughed. Idiot. "Come on, now, Georgie." She hated when he called her that. "I know about your great Aunt Norma passing. And that she left you some property."

Georgia wasn't in the mood to play around. Besides, the shower was running. "How?"

"A little bird told me."

He thought he was funny. "Well, you can't see it, but a little bird is telling you something else right now." She hung up. Maybe he'd heard it from Griff. She wasn't sure. Didn't matter now that Robert knew. That bell couldn't be unrung.

She got in the shower and tried to let the water wash away her new mood. The fact that her phone rang several more times while she was in there didn't help.

At last she got out, wrapped herself and her hair in a towel and did her best to breathe. The phone seemed to have gone silent. Thankfully.

She was just about to walk out the door when it rang again. A different number. She answered it, cautiously. "Hello?"

"Mrs. Carpenter?"

She frowned. Not Robert or Griffin. "Yes. Who's this?"

"Martin Townsend of Townsend, Townsend, and Pulanski."

She sighed. Robert's attorneys. "What do you want?"

"It's about your recent inheritance. We need to take that into consideration for the final divorce decree as it pertains to your net family property. If you could just—"

"My what? You know you're representing a man who broke up his marriage and family by sleeping with the daughter of one of his clients." She wasn't such a gem either, but that was beside the point.

Martin Townsend ignored her. "We need a full accounting of what you inherited. By tomorrow morning, otherwise we'll file an injunction with the judge stating that you're hiding marital assets. Have a good day."

Chapter Twenty-seven

Georgia stared at her phone. If Townsend hadn't hung up, she would have screamed something at him. Something not very nice. Him hanging up had probably saved her some face. But that did nothing to make her feel more charitable toward him.

She was so livid she was trembling. There was only one person she could think of that might be able to help her. It took her two tries to dial the number because her hand was shaking so badly.

The receptionist answered and Georgia was immediately grateful that Mr. Gillum opened his office as early as he did. "Roger Gillum, please. It's Georgia Carpenter and it's urgent."

"Just a moment, Ms. Carpenter."

She waited while the call was transferred.

"Hello, Georgia, it's Roger. What can I do for you?"

She took a breath. "My husband's attorney just called. Somehow, they found out about my inheritance from Norma and they want a full accounting of it. They say they need to take it into consideration for the divorce decree."

"Hmm. I wondered if something like this would happen. Can you send me their information? I'll be happy to handle this."

"You will?"

"Absolutely. I told you I promised Norma I would."

He had said that. She exhaled. "I can't thank you enough."

"Well, don't thank me yet. I need to talk to them first, but I'm pretty sure we can protect everything."

Her panic returned. "Pretty sure?"

"I need to know what their angle is."

"He said something about net family property."

"Hmm." Roger went silent for a few seconds, causing her panic to tick slightly higher. "Interesting. That gives me an idea of what they're thinking. Let me call them and I'll get back to you as soon as possible."

"Thank you."

"You're welcome." He paused. "Would you mind if I looked over whatever they've sent you already? They sound…mercenary, for lack of a better word."

"I'd be happy to show it to you. I can drive it over this morning. In a couple minutes, actually."

"That would be great. I'll text you the address."

"Thanks again."

"We'll solve this, Ms. Carpenter. You'll see."

She hung up, hoping he was right. She sent a quick text to Travis saying she'd be a few minutes late, then gathered everything Robert's attorneys had sent her, pulled on an old sweatshirt, and jumped in the Pathfinder.

The rain was still coming down. Not a downpour, not a drizzle, just a nice steady beat that made the day gloomy and gray. It suited her mood.

She pulled up Roger's texted directions, loaded them into her GPS and headed for his office.

Once she got there, she ran inside and gave the paperwork to his receptionist, Flora. Right after Georgia apologized to her for looking like a homeless person. She explained about working on the inn and the receptionist, a nice older lady, told her not to worry about it. Offered her a cup of coffee, too.

Georgia declined. She was jittery enough already. She said goodbye and hustled back to her SUV.

His office was nice. Not so fancy that anyone would get the impression he was earning too much, but fancy enough to say successful in a reassuring way.

It helped to know he was on her side. If she had to handle this alone…she didn't want to think about that.

She drove straight back to the cottage, parked, then fished an umbrella out of the backseat and made her way to the inn via the sidewalk. She ran up the steps and onto the front porch, where she closed the umbrella, giving it a good shake before she leaned it by the door.

She went in. "Hello?"

"Up here," Travis called. "Blue bathroom."

Second floor. She jogged up the steps. "How's it going?"

"It's…going. Mia's already been here and gone, said she shouldn't be too long."

"I figured." Georgia stuck her head in the blue bathroom and gaped at all the tiles he'd removed from the shower. They were stacked in neat piles on the floor. Almost an entire wall of them. And the wall they'd come off of had been cut away. "Um, this looks like a heck of a lot more than regrouting."

"It is. Unfortunately." He pushed his baseball cap back a little. "I found some rot behind this wall. I'll need to replace the greenboard—"

"The what?"

"It's drywall specifically meant for wet areas. Like this one. And it's not really greenboard anymore, it's cement board but most of us still call it that. For whatever reason, the builder didn't put any behind this section which is why it rotted and looks like this."

"Oh. Good thing you found it, I guess."

"It is." He stood. "I'm about done here. If you want to go with me to the hardware store, I just need a couple minutes."

She nodded. "I do. I want to get paint. What about the other contractor that's coming by to do an estimate?"

His expression turned into annoyance. "They called to reschedule because of the weather."

"Are they made of sugar? Why can't they do an estimate in the rain?"

He shrugged as he let out a little laugh. "Beats me."

She put a hand on her forehead as new frustration bubbled up inside her. Instantly, she made a decision. "Tell Diego he's got the job. Outside only. I don't have time for people who can't keep their appointments."

"You're sure?"

"Yes."

His eyes narrowed. "You're mad about something else. What happened this morning? Bad news from your son?"

She shook her head and leaned on the vanity. "Robert. My ex who isn't my ex yet. He found out about the inn and now he's got his lawyers trying to include it in the divorce."

Travis hissed out a breath. "What a lowlife."

"You can say that again. I think he's doing it to try to get out of alimony. Thankfully, Roger Gillum's looking into it."

"Good. Roger will get to the bottom of it."

She slanted her eyes at Travis. "How well do you know him?"

"Pretty good. I went to high school with his younger brother. Who is a great accountant, by the way."

"Good to know." She smiled. "You know everyone around here, don't you?"

"Not everyone. But yeah, kind of. That's what happens when you grow up in a small town and don't leave."

"Why didn't you? Why didn't you go after your wife and daughter when they moved to Alabama?"

He was silent for a minute. "To be honest, I thought Sam would be crying to come back in a week or two, missing her friends and all that. Didn't happen. And back then, I was too stubborn for my own good. Mad at Jillian, too. Real mad. I thought moving up there would be like admitting I was wrong."

"I get that. I certainly wouldn't have gone after Robert."

"Anyway…" He started straightening up the tools. "Do you know what colors you want?"

"Yes." She hadn't meant to stir up bad memories for him. "I'll pick them out when we get there."

"Okay. Meet you at the truck in a few."

She put her hand on the door frame as she started to leave. "You're a good guy, Travis. Sam's missing out by not having you in her life. And Jillian should be ashamed of herself for letting this go on so long."

He nodded. "Thanks. I mean that. I can be hard on myself sometimes."

"We all can. Human nature." She smiled. "See you at the truck."

They got to the hardware store about twenty minutes later. Travis went off to get greenboard and whatever else he needed, while she headed for the paint department. She stood in front of the chips, mulling over the colors.

There were so many. So. Many.

"Have you decided?"

She looked up to see Travis had appeared next to her. "I only just started."

He laughed. "You've been here fifteen minutes."

"I have?"

"Yep."

She frowned and held out the neutral color samples. "Dust Bunny, Hush, or Bermuda Sand?"

"This is for the bedrooms?"

"Yes."

He stared at the three selections. "Hush looks pink to me."

"Good, me too. I thought I'd just stared at it too long." She stuck that one back.

"Do you have a favorite of those two?"

"I do. But I want to see what you say first."

He narrowed his eyes. "That's not really fair. But despite the name, I like Dust Bunny."

She laughed. "I do too! Dust Bunny it is." She pulled out the kitchen colors. "Now what about these? Cornsilk, Honeybee, or Limitless?"

He screwed up his face. "Limitless? Nothing about that says yellow."

"I didn't name them."

"Limitless is going to come off green in that light. And the name is dumb."

He wasn't wrong. She stuck that one back.

He pointed. "And that's nothing like the color that's actually on a honeybee, but that's my favorite."

"Done. I was leaning toward that one."

"Great. Let's order the paint. If you and Mia help me move furniture and put down tarps, I can start cutting in today."

"Cutting in what?"

He grinned. "The ceiling and around the outlets and…I'll show you. You could even give it a try."

"Deal." She smiled back. "I'm game."

They got the paint and some other supplies for the project, then checked out. Georgia paid with the Sea Glass Inn credit card and they were off.

Her phone rang. Gillum. Her nerves came rushing back.

Maggie Miller

Chapter Twenty-eight

Mia arrived at Bon Voyage Vintage a couple minutes before they opened. She didn't mind waiting in the car, though. It was a chance for the rain to stop. It didn't.

When someone came through the store to the glass front door and flipped the closed sign around, Mia grabbed her purse and made a dash for the entrance.

A bell jangled as she came in. "Morning. I'm Mia Carpenter. I talked to someone yesterday about donating some of my aunt's things?"

"Oh, yes." The woman behind the counter smiled. "I'm Agatha Goodwin. I spoke to you. Nice to meet you, Mia."

"Thanks, you too. Do you want me to just bring everything in or do you have a back entrance?"

"We do, but if you're parked out front no need to move. Front door is fine." She peered through the glass storefront at the rain. "Dreadful weather though."

"It is, but everything's in plastic bags so it should be fine."

"Would you like some help?"

Mia didn't want the older lady getting wet. Her hair looked like it had just been set. "Nope. I can manage just fine. No need for us both to get wet."

"That's very kind of you."

Mia hauled everything in. Three trips. Which left her pretty soaked.

Agatha handed her a wad of paper towels off a roll from under the counter. "You poor thing. You're drenched."

"I'll dry." But Mia smiled as she dabbed at her face. "I tried to go through everything and weed out the things that were too worn to be useful, but if you find anything that's not suitable, feel free to throw it out."

"I'm sure it'll all be fine. We thank you for the generous donation. Let me just get you a receipt."

"There will be probably be more coming."

Agatha's expression turned curious. "Who was your aunt?"

"Norma Merriweather."

Agatha's mouth rounded in a little, surprised O. "These are Norma's things?"

"Yes, ma'am."

"Oh my. Well, these are special then, aren't they?"

"They are?"

"Certainly." Agatha came around and started pulling the bags off to one side. "Norma was a very good friend and a dear member of this community. We all loved her very much. Well…not all of us, perhaps. But those of us who weren't morally compromised."

Mia rolled her lips in to keep from laughing. She was going to have to tell her mom about that one. Morally compromised. "You must be talking about Laverne. No, wait, Lavinia, right?"

"Right." Agatha's penciled on brows arched. "So you know about her?"

"I've heard stories. Is she still around?"

"She is. She's on the town council now, believe it or not. As for those stories, well, some of them are true. Some of them aren't."

"Really? How can I tell the difference?"

"Well…" Agatha seemed to think that over. "You just come ask me. Or one of the other girls from the bridge club. We'll tell you."

"There's a bridge club?"

"There was. Things sort of petered off after Norma got sick and closed the inn. We used to meet there every Tuesday afternoon for our game. We tried meeting at our houses, but it wasn't the same."

Mia leaned on the counter. "Tell you what. You tell me if a story I've heard is true, and I'll tell you some good news."

Agatha's eyes sparkled. "Oh, that sounds like a fair trade. What story have you heard?"

Mia took a shot. "That my aunt got approval for the third floor of the inn because she had a *special* relationship with the councilman who made it happen."

"She absolutely did. They were going together, you know."

That wasn't quite what Mia was trying to get verified. "So she…and he were…you know…"

Agatha gasped. "You mean that kind of special. Heavens, no." She leaned in closer, like she was about to reveal a big secret. "But that's what your aunt wanted people to think. The truth is she paid for Herb Sorenson's dog to have its broken leg fixed."

"What?"

Agatha nodded, straightening. "Norma was at the vet with Jeff, her cat before Clyde, when Herb came in with Hambone. Hambone had been hit by a car and the poor creature was in bad shape. Herb thought he was going to have to put him down. The surgery was a king's ransom."

Agatha shook her head slowly. "Norma paid the bill. With the agreement that he never tell a soul. After that they started dating and the rumor about how she got that third floor just grew out of that. And she let people believe it. Said it added to her mystique."

"Wow." Mia chuckled softly. "She wasn't wrong."

Agatha's smile was proud. "Norma was an amazing woman. We miss her very much."

"My mom does too. Unfortunately, I never really got to know her."

"That is unfortunate. You would have loved her. And her you, I'm sure. So…" Agatha's eyes twinkled. "What's the good news?"

Mia's smile broadened. "My mom and I are reopening the inn. And you and the girls are welcome to come over and play bridge whenever you like once we get open."

Agatha's face lit up and she pressed her hands together in front of her. "That *is* great news. I'm so glad it's staying in the family. And I can't wait to tell the girls."

Mia loved how happy the news made her. "Well, I should go. Tons to do."

"Sweetheart, if you need anything, you just call me, you hear?"

"Yes, ma'am. I'll be back later with the second load."

"See you then." Agatha was already reaching for the phone.

Mia just grinned as she left and headed to Ludlows for the boxes she needed to finish packing up the bedrooms. Word about them reopening the inn would spread now. Hopefully, that would bring them some business too. And it might also help some of Mia's other plans that were going to require community participation.

When she got back to the inn, she found her mom and Travis working in Aunt Norma's bedroom.

"Hey," she said, looking over the armful of flattened boxes she was carrying. "I wasn't quite done in here. Are you guys going to paint?

"We're just prepping," her mom answered. "You still have time to finish up. How much longer do you think you need?"

"I have to box up all the stuff on the bed and then all the small things that are going into storage. Maybe an hour."

"We have to do the second bedroom after this so you should be fine." Travis was setting up a ladder. "Anything that's in the nightstands or dressers can stay. We're going to move most of the furniture to the middle and cover it with drop cloths."

"I've already cleaned out the dresser," Mia said. "Except for the drawers with the jewelry."

"It'll be fine to stay in there for now. If you want."

"Yeah, that would be one less thing for me to do." Mia started putting one of the boxes together. "Rats. I need packing tape to secure these. I didn't think about that."

"Should be some in the pantry," Travis said. "Look by where the toolbox is kept. If not, I'm sure I have a roll or two at my house."

Mia headed off to the pantry. The tape was right where Travis said it would be.

She got to work taping up boxes, then put her efforts into overdrive to fill them and finish cleaning out the two rooms. Aunt Norma's room took the longest as the other room had very little in it to be removed.

Travis and her mom kept working around her. They taped things up, covered things over with tarps, and did whatever else was necessary to prep the rooms for paint.

Mia kept all the designer things in the closet. There was no reason to move them out just yet. The rest of the things to be donated she packed into the boxes, then carried them out to her car, filling the trunk, the backseat, and even ending up with one box on her passenger seat up front.

A light drizzle was still coming down.

Her mom had helped her carry the last few out and now stood by the car. "Are you taking them over to the thrift shop now?"

"I was going to. Unless you need me for something?"

"No, I think Travis and I will get to work on the painting."

"Oh, that reminds me. The lady at the thrift shop, Agatha, she was a friend of Aunt Norma's. A good one, by the sounds of it. They were part of a group of women who used to play bridge here every Tuesday."

"Here at the inn?"

Mia nodded. "I hope it's all right, but I told them they could come back and do that again once we got opened."

"Of course it's all right." Georgia smiled. "It would be nice to have them. If nothing else it would make the inn seem busy if it's not."

"I think it will be. But I like the idea of the community feeling like the inn could be a gathering place of sorts, you know? That sort of thing will only help us. I feel."

Georgia nodded. "You're very right, it will. Good job."

Mia smiled. "Agatha told me something else. The real story about how Aunt Norma got that third floor."

"Oh?" Georgia leaned on the top of the car. "I'm surprised a little old lady would tell those kinds of stories."

Mia snorted. "Mom, it's nothing like that. Basically, she helped Herb, the councilman, pay a vet bill for his dog, which saved the dog's life. That's why they started dating. She swore him to secrecy about it, but he repaid her with that third floor. The other story is just a rumor she let spread because she thought it made her sound like a character."

"Well, it did. And she was anyway." Georgia shook her head. "How about that."

"Right? I think Agatha will be a good one to stay in touch with. She said if we needed anything to let her know." Mia glanced up. The drizzle had finally stopped. "She's very excited we're reopening the inn."

"How nice of her." Georgia looked pleased. "Nothing wrong with a little local support. I look forward to meeting her."

"You want to come with me to drop off this stuff?"

"I'd love to, but I don't want to leave Travis by himself to paint. He's supposed to be teaching me how to cut in."

Mia made a face. "Which is what?"

"A painting thing. Hey, if you can learn to change toilet valves, I should learn something too, right?"

Mia laughed. "Right. Okay, be back soon."

She would be too. But not before she had another talk with Agatha. The woman was going to be a valuable resource and that alone was enough to give Mia all kinds of new and interesting ideas for promoting the inn.

Ideas she would very soon be presenting to her mother.

Chapter Twenty-nine

Georgia learned how to cut in with such speed and accuracy that she earned a surprised look from Travis. "What?" she said. "It's not that hard. In fact, it's a lot like icing a cake. Something I used to do pretty regularly."

"Were you a baker?" he asked.

"Sort of." She carefully outlined the door frame with paint, making sure to keep the line of Dust Bunny beige nice and straight and not overlapping the white trim.

"What does that mean?" He was up on the ladder, cutting in the ceiling.

"I had a little home baking business for about a minute. Mostly birthday cakes, cupcakes for kids' parties, stuff like that. Did a couple of anniversary cakes, another one for a retirement, and more graduation cupcakes than I can count. But the attorney's bills for the divorce were too much. I was forced to move to a small studio apartment and the kitchen was practically non-existent. I had to give up the business."

"I'm sorry to hear that."

"Thanks. The inn couldn't have come along at a better time."

"You know, you could offer custom cakes here. For the guests, I mean. A lot of people used to come here to celebrate anniversaries. Other things too, I'm sure, but anniversaries are the ones I remember most. Norma used to keep a couple bottles of champagne in the fridge all the time just for those special occasions."

"That's a great idea. We need to do that too. The champagne, I mean. But I love the cake idea as well." She smiled as she worked. "I'll have to think about that. See how busy I am with actual inn business. Maybe I could do it. If I had enough notice."

They worked all day. Mia joined them when she returned. And because they were working so hard, they didn't break for lunch, opting to order a pizza instead.

The rain came back, too. After Travis finished eating, he went upstairs to check on the roof where he'd repaired it.

He was smiling when he came down. "Looks good. Not that I had any doubts, but still nice to have the visual reassurance."

"Excellent." Georgia hadn't had any doubts either. Travis didn't strike her as the kind of person who cut any corners in his work.

They got back to painting and finished both rooms a little after sunset. The rain was still drizzling down. They were too exhausted to care.

Travis got to work on closing up the five-gallon bucket of paint. "With the humidity, these walls might take a bit longer to dry. I wouldn't plan on moving in just yet."

"No problem," Georgia said. "We aren't in a rush."

Mia rolled her shoulders. "Tomorrow we do the kitchen?"

Travis nodded. "Mostly you two until I get that bathroom fixed upstairs. Although I'm not sure that wall will be dry by then. This humidity makes that tough. Anyway, with all three of us, the kitchen should go pretty fast. More cutting in, though. And more taping up to do. It's a big room."

"At least we don't have to worry about the floor," Georgia said.

"Why not?" Mia asked.

Georgia realized she'd forgot to tell Mia. "The hardware store had some tiles on close out. Those kinds that look like wood planks but are actually ceramic? With Travis's builder discount we were able to get enough to redo the kitchen floor for less than really nice linoleum would have been."

"That's fantastic. What color?"

Georgia laughed. "Probably not a very popular one since it was on sale, but I thought it would look nice. It's a like a whitewashed grayish driftwood color."

Mia tipped her head. "With the white cabinets and new pale-yellow walls, it actually sounds like it'll be perfect. It is a beach house, after all."

"Your mom got a light fixture too."

Georgia nodded. "Also on sale. Just a simple brushed nickel fan and light combination. But it's much more modern than that florescent that's in there now."

"I can't wait to see it all," Mia said.

"And I can't wait for a shower and a beer." Travis finished gathering up the tools, looked at them both, and started laughing.

"What?" Georgia said.

He shook his head. "You two have a lot of paint on you."

"Do we?" Mia looked at her mom. "Do I?"

Georgia made a face. "Kiddo, if I look like you do, we are going to have to scrub hard when we shower tonight."

"Well," Mia said. "You're pretty covered. I mean, it's in your hair and everything."

"You too." Georgia tried not to laugh. "Eh, who cares. Tomorrow we'll be adding some yellow to the beige, so what's the big deal?"

"Exactly." Mia looked around. "What else do we need to do to clean up and go home?"

"I've got it," Travis said. "You two go on."

"You're sure?" Georgia asked. "We don't mind helping. We can wash out brushes or whatever."

Travis glanced at her, clearly thinking about her offer. "Okay. If you guys want to wash the brushes, that would be fine. Use the sink in the laundry room."

"What about the rollers?" Mia asked.

Travis shook his head. "I'm throwing them out. We'll have new ones for tomorrow."

"Sounds good." Georgia took the brushes they'd used and headed for the laundry and the big sink in there.

Mia followed, taking one of the brushes from her as she turned the water on. "Long day, but a good day. Those rooms already look so much different."

"They do," Georgia said as she worked the paint out of the bristles. Seemed like an endless supply no matter how much she rinsed the brush.

"So, Mom, question."

Georgia knew that tone. Mia was excited about something. "Yes?"

"What do you think about really pushing the wedding angle? I mean like trying to get us in some wedding guides, stuff like that?"

"I think that sounds great, but I don't know that we can really compete with the bigger locations. And we don't have the kind of stuff you need for an outdoor set up. Chairs, canopies, all of that."

"But we could get all of that. Or find a rental company and work out a package with them." She shrugged. "Something like that."

"We could. What else have you been thinking about?"

Mia took a breath. "Okay, don't shoot it down just yet but I was thinking about having a wedding cake contest. We could host it here and get the local media involved, plus I talked to Lucas and he said Ludlows would definitely help sponsor it and they could offer their head baker as a judge."

"Wow. You've been busy."

She nodded and went on. "Since I found the top tier of Aunt Norma's cake, I was thinking we could preserve it and make it part of the presentation. Maybe even invite a bridal shop to show a few of their dresses and again, we could use Aunt Norma's dress as an inspiration for all of this."

Georgia smiled at the idea. It would be a lovely tribute to the woman who'd made it all possible "I love this. All of it. I especially love the idea of Aunt Norma being the inspiration. Good job."

"Yeah?"

Georgia nodded. "Yeah."

Mia grinned. "Thanks. I feel like I can get a lot of play out of it on social media too."

"Sounds good to me. Just tell me what you need."

"Will you make a cake?"

"Me? A wedding cake?" She'd done a small one once. Nothing all that fancy. "I don't know."

"Come on, Mom. You wouldn't have to include it in the judging, but I think it would be cool for you to participate as the new innkeeper."

Georgia shook the water from her brush. "I'll think about it, okay? But it might be better for me to be one of the judges."

"Okay. I'll keep organizing and see how it goes." Mia pressed her brush against the sink to get the water out. "I think that's as clean as it's going to get."

"Same here. Let's go home and collapse."

"You know that's right. I'm not sure I have the energy to eat dinner."

Georgia chuckled. "We still have some of that chocolate silk pie left."

"I have enough energy for that."

Travis stuck his head in. "You guys want me to drive you to your cottage? It's still raining pretty good."

Georgia shook her head. "We're just going to shower anyway. But thank you."

"Yeah, thanks," Mia said.

"All right. See you in the morning."

"Night," they both said.

They went through the house, making sure the lights were off, then Georgia locked the front door behind them. They stood on the front porch for a moment.

Mia sighed. "It's not going to let up. We should just go."

"Agreed. And at least we have the umbrella to share." Georgia opened it up, then Mia got under it with her and they started down the steps.

The umbrella was really meant for one, so the rain still got them. As they exited the front gate, they both broke into a jog that lasted until they reached their own porch.

They were both laughing as they went inside. Georgia pulled off her wet sweatshirt, but her t-shirt was still damp underneath. "What do you say we shower, then meet in the living room for a little mindless television and pie?"

"There's nothing I want to do more," Mia said. "Just as soon as I put out dinner for Clyde. If he's not too mad at being cooped up in here all day."

Georgia laughed. "I'm sure dinner will cheer him up."

"No doubt. He loves his food."

And twenty minutes later, they were all in the living room. Pie and wine on the coffee table for Georgia and Mia who were both in their pajamas and robes. They had a gameshow on the television, and Clyde was sprawled next to Mia on the couch, cleaning his fur. Mia had put the towel there for him to lay on in an effort to keep some fur off the cushion. It was helping. A little.

Georgia was tired but content. And happy. Progress was being made. What more could she ask for? A little sadness crept in to dampen her mood. Her son. That's what more she could ask for. But there wasn't anything she could do about that. She sipped her wine. He was his own man, living his own life. He'd get in touch when he was ready.

A knock at the door made her turn, although she couldn't see the door from where she was sitting.

Mia looked too. "Who could that be?"

Clyde didn't move.

"Maybe Travis?" Georgia put her glass down to check her phone. There was no message from him. "I'll go check. I really hope the roof isn't leaking again. But with this weather, who knows?"

She tightened the belt of her robe as she went to the door and opened it. A gasp slipped from her lips. Standing there, wet from the rain, was Griffin.

And he had a baby in his arms.

Want to know when Maggie's next book comes out? Then don't forget to sign up for her newsletter at her website!

Also, if you enjoyed the book, please recommend it to a friend. Even better yet, leave a review and let others know.

Other Books by Maggie Miller:

Gulf Coast Cottage
Gulf Coast Secrets
Gulf Coast Reunion
Gulf Coast Sunsets
Gulf Coast Moonlight
Gulf Coast Promises
Gulf Coast Wedding
Gulf Coast Christmas

Maggie Miller

About Maggie:

Maggie Miller thinks time off is time best spent at the beach, probably because the beach is her happy place. The sound of the waves is her favorite background music, and the sand between her toes is the best massage she can think of.

When she's not at the beach, she's writing or reading or cooking for her family. All of that stuff called life.

She hopes her readers enjoy her books and welcomes them to drop her a line and let her know what they think!

Maggie Online:

www.maggiemillerauthor.com
www.facebook.com/MaggieMillerAuthor

Made in the USA
Las Vegas, NV
12 February 2024

85663976R00138